QUEER LIFE, QUEER LOVE

Edited by Matt Bates
and Golnoosh Nour

MUSWELL
PRESS

First published by Muswell Press in 2021

Typeset in Bembo by M Rules
Printed and bound by CPI Group (UK) Ltd, Croydon CR0 4YY

Introduction copyright © Matt Bates & Golnoosh Nour 2021

A CIP catalogue record for this book is available from the British Library

ISBN: 978-1-83811-016-1
eISBN: 978-1-83811-017-8

Muswell Press
London N6 5HQ
www.muswell-press.co.uk

Publisher's Note
Sarah and Kate would like to thank everyone involved in this Anthology
for their time and their wonderful work. Particular thanks to Matt Bates
and Golnoosh Nour, Fiona Brownlee, Jamie Keenan, and Laura
McFarlane. Lucy would be delighted that the book we
talked about 2 years ago is now a reality.

7 9 10 8 6

Lucy
1999–2020

Contents

Introduction

When, in March 2020, we received the devastating news of the death of Lucy Reynolds, publisher Sarah Beal's trans daughter, we both felt immense grief. Neither of us had met Lucy in person, nor did we have any interactions with her, so whilst our grief stemmed from our compassion for Sarah's loss, it was intensified by the fact that this was another lost queer life.

Being queer is hard. Recognising one's own personal difference and learning self-acceptance can be a painful and bewildering journey. And it is more than just identifying as LGBTQ+. To us, queerness is about disrupting the status quo. While identifying as anything other than cis-heterosexual is automatically disruptive to the cis-heteronormative world that we have to live in, queerness is also about an attitude, and a courage that lets one express their own deviation from the norm. Writing is an action, a call to arms. Putting words on the page, articulating our fears and desires is a form of resistance: a symbolic shredding of the heteronormative script.

We received hundreds of submissions from almost every corner of the world and with so many amazingly written queer texts, the final selection process was tough. In the end, we decided on entries not only representative of many races, genders, and sexualities in all their rainbow glories, but also those that we found sublime and extraordinary in regard to literary craft. In this sense, we were interested in not just pushing the boundaries of gender and sexuality, but also the boundaries of literature itself. That's why we specified in the submission call out that we were interested in both poetry and prose, short stories, narrative non-fiction or indeed a hybrid of these. Although each entry was submitted independently, as we began the selection process a glorious sense of continuity and community began to emerge. Words and sentences created in private, in those liminal spaces where despair and desire meet, are articulated here and expand upon queer difference, queer difficulty, queer curiosity, and solidarity. These works shout, demand and proclaim our capacity to express queer life and queer love.

This beautifully daring collection is to honour a young, lost, queer life, but also to create more space to encourage and salute the diversity of queer writing, and to celebrate the richness of queer life experience.

Golnoosh & Matt
Autumn 2021

In Mercy and with Faith –
Katlego Kai Kolanyane-Kesupile

For I did not come to hate the word
h/H/**H**/HeeEe
instead I (simply) chose the door where
it could be unbridled
to think itself free

no knees for engagements
or hairy palms
from spoiling seed

no braver than when help
could be sought and granted
and tears dove in lullaby streams
and disappeared – when dreams
could still be sweet

no muscle better than
the beating of a heart
against an ear

a rush of time fast
slow and clear

if I come bare
in arms
they are a shaking horizon
glittered by a waving sun

I did (not) come here
to hate
in stead, I surrendered
your fight, stayed
Hermetic and took flight.

For in All I can be   *Mer   cy*
For in All I can find more   *Faith*
than settle in aboard
an ark. With no course
death
gallops in fields of sorrow.

Katlego Kai Kolanyane-Kesupile is an international award-winning Cultural Architect and Development Practitioner from Botswana with imprints in education, communications and human rights. Her work centres on decoloniality, feminism and disability theory. Her writing ranges from contemporary critiques, creative work in poetry, music and theatre, and scholarly research. Katlego holds an MA in Human Rights, Culture and Social Justice from Goldsmiths University of London.

How to Build an Identity Without an Essence – Jonathan Kemp

'Behind the permitted words, listen for the others!'
–Jean Genet

If 'sexual identity is a narrative we tell ourselves and we tell about ourselves' (Hall, 2009, p.1), then queer narratives, like queer selves, cannot fail to twist, interrupt and trouble the established modes of storytelling. Queer transverses and traverses – crosses and crosses out – all the bog-standard (straight, in every sense of the word) ways of being and telling: queering the pitch because we must. Because content is form, form content.

To define is to limit and as such queer must never be defined, yet strategic essentialism (Spivak) demands that I do, that I name the unnameable, describe the ineluctable. Yet we must never forget that something about queer *is* inextinguishable, inexhaustible; that ineffability is part of what it is: without it, queer isn't queer. There must always be a certain unintelligibility at work in queer's work, for it is an identity without an essence (Halperin).

Since its reappropriation/reclamation in the early 1990s as a critical and disruptive force rather than a stinging insult, queer has been a highly contentious word: a battle-field, semantic or otherwise, rather than a straightforward descriptor or noun. But the contentious nature of the word, I would argue, is its very purpose, even its nature, if one could risk claiming it had such a thing. This verbing of a noun has ruffled and must continue to ruffle as many feathers as possible, undermine all certainties, set orthodoxies quivering. As a verb, it reverberates through the corridors of academe, like Jesus tipping the money-lenders' tables, every department overrun and overturned. The most august of our institutions have been exposed and accused; every gallery, theatre and pleasure dome is a bloodbath of sexual politics, a steaming orgy of queer. It's wishful thinking, of course, but what else is left once the imagination's been ransacked, lobotomised by the internal pressure of conformity, but to balance on the tightrope of lunacy and art?

Replace existence with the desire to exist.

Queer always has its legs and eyes wide open, knowing that discursive whoring will get you everywhere. Queer has opened up its arms and said *'mmmmm yes'* a million times. Like all good cynics, its heart is there, on its sleeve, for all to see. These words: queer thinking, queer theory, queer lives, queer loves are cornerstones demarking a rich territory of consciousness and feeling, testaments to what it is to be – here and now – thinking and living and loving queerly, as a queer, as someone who queers, someone queered.

In 1993, Judith Butler wrote:

> The assertion of 'queer' will be necessary as a term
> of affiliation, but it will not fully describe those it

purports to represent. As a result, it will be necessary to affirm the contingency of the term: to let it be vanquished by those who are excluded by the term but who justifiably expect representation by it, to let it take on means that cannot now be anticipated by a younger generation whose political vocabulary may well carry a very different set of investments (Butler 1993, p.230).

Because queer comes with its own criteria, is its own criteria, as such we can't use pre-established criteria to recognise it, let alone judge it. If it names anything, it names a critical energy or impulse that can never – must never – settle.

References

Judith Butler, *Bodies That Matter: On the Discursive Limits of Sex,* Routledge 1993

Donald Hall, *Reading Sexualities: Hermeneutic Theory and the Future of Queer Studies,* Routledge, 2009

Jonathan Kemp's debut novel *London Triptych* won the Authors' Club Best First Novel Award.

The Guardian called it 'an ambitious, fast-moving, and sharply written work' and *Time Out* called it 'a thoroughly absorbing and pacy read'. His next book, *Twentysix* (2011), was a collection of queer erotic prose poems. A second novel, *Ghosting,* appeared in March 2015. His non-fiction includes *The Penetrated Male*, (Punctum Books 2012) and, *Homotopia? Gay Identity, Sameness & the Politics of Desire* in 2016. He teaches creative writing at Middlesex University. More info on his website: jonathan-kemp.com

My Name is Frida – Rosy Adams

My parents christened me 'Alfie'. I hate it, just as I hated
the dull colours of my boy's clothes and the hard, angular
toys they bought for me. They took me to football club
after school, even though it was obvious that I hated that
too. Dad would drag me outside for a kick-about on Sunday
afternoons and I would try my best, but I wasn't fooling
anyone, least of all myself.

I want to be an artist. They think it's a waste of time.
You'll never make a living from poncing about with a paintbrush.
Dad's words. Even so, they make sure I never go short of
art materials. It may not be what they'd prefer, but I think
they were relieved when I found something, anything, that
I really wanted to do.

He tries to hide it, but I know Dad is disappointed in
me. It must be hard for him. We don't have anything in
common at all. One time, I overheard him say to Mum,

'Well, at least he isn't gay. He's always after hanging
round the girls.'

Mum didn't reply. She doesn't say much, but she doesn't
miss much either.

My best friend is Fran. She's the only one who really

gets me. I go round her house and we dress up and do each other's make-up with a chair wedged against her door so none of her brothers or sisters can come in. She says she wishes that she was an only child, like me, but it's not as great as she thinks.

Last year Ms Arlington (my art teacher, who tells us to call her 'Jen') introduced me to Frida Kahlo. I fell in love with everything about her. She said, *I used to think I was the strangest person in the world but then I thought there are so many people in the world, there must be someone just like me who feels bizarre and flawed in the same ways I do. I would imagine her, and imagine that she must be out there thinking of me too. Well, I hope that if you are out there and read this and know that, yes, it's true I'm here, and I'm just as strange as you.*

I cried when I read it. It was like she was talking directly to me. That's why I named myself for her, because she made me realise who I really am. She's the one who gave me the confidence to start showing myself to the world. I don't care if some of the other kids laugh at me, and even some of the teachers give me the side eye. I've got Fran, and I've got Frida.

Sam. I watch him from out of the corners of my eyes, or through my fringe so he looks fuzzy and dreamy. Not moving my head to look. Not catching the eyes of the others, who would tease me.

He's always restless in class. He tosses his head, flicking the hair out of his eyes, and twitching his shoulders from one position to the next.

I catalogue him in secret. At rest, smoking a roll-up out the back, hips cocked and resting his weight on one foot. In P.E., running up and down the football field, not much for kicking the ball, just racing up and down, laughing, long legs flicking mud and grass everywhere. Once, angry, arguing with another boy, his head thrown back and teeth showing, and his voice ringing out a challenge.

At night I imagine him with me. The feel of his taut, springy muscle under my hands. Warm breath on the nape of my neck.

Who am I kidding? He doesn't even know I exist.

My hands are shaking, but the outfit I've chosen has no pockets, so I fold my arms tight across my chest. I have to walk slowly because I'm not used to walking out in heels. I've practised in the house, but it's not the same. The clack of them hitting the pavement sounds way too loud.

I can see Fran up ahead. She's waiting for me at the entrance to the arcade. Even though she's seen me dressed like this, she has to look twice before she recognises me.

'Wow! You look amazing.'

'Really?'

'Really.'

We link arms and walk along the Prom. The tide is in and the breakers are throwing spray and sand over the railings. I can see the boys at the end of the wooden jetty, playing chicken with the waves. The setting sun turns them into shadow puppets, but even so I can pick him out with one glance.

I look away.

I make myself breathe in deep through my nose, like the counsellor told me, concentrating on the reek of seaweed and chips.

We stroll, Fran and I, putting on our best *whatever* faces.

They notice us, and we are showered with wolf whistles and ape noises. But not him. He's not looking at us. He's mooching around at the back of the group, peering into the water.

Steffan, his best mate, shouts to Fran, 'Hey Fran! Who's your friend?'

They haven't recognised me. I don't know how to respond, but Fran calls back, 'Ask her yourself!'

And we strut past, swaying our hips and pretending to ignore them.

The next day, at school, Steffan sits next to me at break.

'That was you, yesterday, wasn't it? With Fran?'

I nod, keeping my eyes down, bracing myself for the anger and the ridicule that I know is coming.

'I just wanted to say, I thought you looked really nice.'

I did not expect that.

'Thanks. That means a lot.'

He stands up. Smiles. Says, 'Yeah, uh, like I said, I just wanted to let you know.'

He trips over his bag, catches himself on the chair, and walks away.

After that, Steffan starts to hang out with me and Fran at break times. To begin with, I'm hopeful that he'll bring Sam with him, but he's always busy with something or other. Still, it's nice to have another friend that accepts me for who I am. I'm lucky, I suppose.

One day, we start talking about crushes. It seems like Fran has a new one every week, and she's not shy about it. Steffan admits to liking someone but he won't tell us who it is, even when we pin him down and tickle him without mercy. He rolls around on the floor, protesting, 'Stop, I can't breathe, I can't breathe!'

Then I tell them about Sam.

They're quiet for a bit too long.

'What? Is that bad?'

'No, no, it's just that, uh . . .' Fran stops, looking awkward.

Steffan says, 'Frida, you know Sam's gay, right?'

No. I didn't know that.

Frida looks down at me from the uneven framing of white printer paper. She appears inscrutable, despite the harsh tracery of thorn covering her chest and shoulders. She seems to say, *I live with pain. I'm used to it.* Near it is another printout; in it she's bound and exposed, fractured but still whole, and pierced all over: Christ like, with nails.

I pray to her for guidance. *What do I do now?* I feel like my world has fractured. I thought he would love me when he realised I wasn't a boy. Only to find out he preferred boys all along.

I run down to the kitchen. In the cupboard under the sink is a roll of black bin bags. I rip off a couple and return to my room. I pull drawers from their runners, emptying the gorgeous, feminine paraphernalia straight into a rubbish sack. Frida stares at my activity with disapproval. I take her pictures and lay their faces down with care on the dressing table. That will have to go too. Boys don't have dressing tables. But not right now. The make-up, hair things, and perfumes sitting on top go straight into another bag. Air whooshes out when I tie the top of the bag. It smells of flowers and wax.

When I'm finished there's not much left. Just one small bottle of nail polish in cobalt blue, the same colour as the Frida's *Casa Azul*. I hide it in the back of a drawer.

I heave the bags down the stairs, out the back, and into

the wheelie bin. On the way back to my room I take a pair of scissors from the kitchen. I sit at my dressing table and look into the mirror. I pick one of Frida's self-portraits and turn it face up, like a tarot card. It is *Self-portrait with cropped hair*. She looks at me sideways, with a small, bitter smile, ugly hanks of hair discarded at her feet.

Deep breath. I can do this.

In the morning I sit down at the table and keep my eyes on my bowl of cereal. Dad says,

'I wish you'd make up your bloody mind!' and slams the door on his way out of the house.

Mum says nothing, as usual, just looks hard at my bare face and tufty hair. She turns away and starts scrubbing the cooker with unnecessary force.

It's Monday.

At school, even though our uniform is fairly sexless, people notice, and pretend they haven't noticed.

I don't care. There's only one person who I want to notice me. And he does! He looks at me for a full five seconds, raises his beautiful straight brows and smiles; then turns back to his friends and says something I can't hear. The friends laugh and turn to look at me as well. Apart from Steffan, who has a moody scowl on his face. I smile at them all and walk to class, reminding myself not to sway my hips.

'Oh my God!'

It's Fran.

'Frida, *wtf*?'

I forgot all about Fran. This is going to be really awkward.

'I'm not Frida anymore.'

'What? *Why?*'

'I've, uh, changed my mind.'

'You can't just change your mind about your identity! What happened? Is someone bullying you?'

'No, look, can we talk about this later?'

People are beginning to stare at us.

'OK, "Alfie".'

She walks away and I flinch at the sound of my birth name. It sounds wrong. But I'll get used to it. He's worth it.

After school I see Sam slouching at the bus stop, alone. I run my fingers through what's left of my hair and I walk over to him.

'Hi.'

He glances at me.

'Hey.'

His eyes return to their contemplation of the pavement.

'I'm Alfie.'

'Yeah? I thought your name was "Frida".'

'Not anymore. It was a phase. I'm over it.'

'Whatever you say.'

He yawns. Slides his feet outwards until he's sitting on the pavement. Pulls out a baccy pouch and starts making a roll-up.

'You smoke?'

'Uh, no.'

He shrugs.

'So what do you do for fun, "Alfie"?'

'Um, I don't know. I suppose I need to find some new hobbies.'

He smiles at that.

'I was wondering ... I thought maybe, you might like to go out sometime?'

'Like a date?'

I'm breathless. I squeeze out a tiny 'yes'.

'Look Alfie, don't take this the wrong way, but you're not my type.'

'I could . . .'

'No, you couldn't. I'm seeing someone.'

'Who?'

He lights up. Inhales. Holds the breath for a moment. Lets go. The name sighs out of his mouth with the smoke.

'Richard Sweetman. He's on the football team.'

'But . . . I thought . . .'

'Like I said, you're not my type.'

The bus pulls up. He offers me the roll-up.

'Here. You look like you need it.'

I take it without thinking and he steps onto the bus and disappears up the stairs to the top deck.

The driver asks if I want to get on. I shake my head, and the bus shudders away. I raise the roll-up to my lips but it's already gone out.

Is this how Frida felt, after Diego betrayed her? Did she sit in her room, turning her face to the shadowed corner, replaying the moment he walked away? All the pain she suffered: how did she never try to kill herself?

I am not Frida. I am not so strong.

Mum tries to talk to me. I won't let her in. She gives up eventually.

Fran messages me at least twenty times. I don't answer.

There's another knock on my bedroom door.

'Just go away, Mum. I don't want to talk about it!'

'It's me. Steffan.'

What's Steffan doing here?

'Can we talk?'

I open the door. He walks into my room, asks if he can sit down. He takes the bed. I sit by the dressing table.

'What do you want to talk about?'

'Sam told me, about you asking him out.'

I can't look at him.

'Frida . . .'

'Don't call me that!'

'You're Frida, more than you'll ever be Alfie! Stop trying to be something you're not.'

I put my hands over my face. I can't bear him to see me.

'I really like you, Frida.'

'Even like this?' I grab the tufts of my hair and pull it, tears stinging my eyes.

'Yes.'

'What does that make you then? Are you gay or straight? Or do you have to be bi to like someone like me?'

He looks down at his feet, blushing.

'I don't know . . . does it matter?'

I go and sit next to him on the bed.

He takes my hand. Leans in to me. Kisses me right on the lips, as carefully as if I were a newly emerged butterfly.

No. It doesn't matter at all.

Rosy Adams is a Welsh writer and therapist who lives in the seaside town of Aberystwyth with her family. She is currently working on producing and editing a new online magazine.

Amethyst – Richard Scott

After Rimbaud

Here they come! Lorries dense with lilac lads – Marys
posing in purple spandex – puce puppies and piss-slaves and
pierced twinks – amethyst-wigged drag queens serving face,
body – daddies painted in mulberry leathers! A hundred
floats sparkling and catching the light like split-open geode
clusters, glitter and feathers raining down.

And coffins, crystalline and shining, raised high on
chiselled shoulders – and jam-velvet canopies sewn with
semi-precious stones twinkling like the starry skies of
your village childhood – and painted placards and lavender
badges and pink triangles, vibrational. O amethyst, stone of
transmutation – centring and violet-bright – all this energy
becomes love, soothing and self-soothing. Our veins are
tinted purple!

And mares, massive and iris-skinned, their legs and
flanks stretching down from the amethyst empyrean. Our
feathered caps are stroking their furred and calming bellies,
low-ceiling and periwinkle safety.

No one of us are damaged. No burning, molten attrition, mantle's pressure here – just this effervescence – the continuation of light – retina and optic nerve disco. Amethyst is living iron and single point scrying – prismatic absolute protector!

Even our ruts, pure amethyst-fire and burnished, as we round the bend –

Richard Scott was born in London in 1981. His publications include *Soho* (Faber & Faber, 2018).

A History of Sheds – Jon Ransom

Sunlight can be surprising. Before, in his shed, a chunk of bright light poured through the broken windowpane. He cleared a space for me on the stained workbench to put my back against. Piling empty pots, thick with green, on the floor. I had given him a condom he turned over in his palm like a shiny coin dug out of the dirt. I pulled down my trackie bottoms and underpants together, left bunched around wet trainers.

Then we were away. Beneath me the bench yawned, surprised by the shifting. Keen as anything, I told him, 'Steady on.' After a while, light from the window hitting my hard-on hypnotised me, casting a clever shadow angled towards my hip, trying to tell the time. There is a wonder to sunlight.

Now we are digging ground beneath October sky, because this is our routine. He instructs me on the way of dirt, big black chunks hard with cold. I am to leave the clods unbroken for winter to freeze, spring to thaw. These trenches have given me a palmful of blisters, an ache in my shoulders I seesaw to loosen.

If I stop and look up, Campbell's brick tower won't be

there, coughing clouds all over the place. They blew it down this summer past. And now I am here on his allotment, with no place else to be, a herd of sheds grazing in the mud behind us. Cold but for the heat in my backside still hanging there.

'Simon—'

I don't know why he calls me this, as it is not my name. Though I like the way Simon sounds as if he is saying *someone*. 'What?' and leave off shovelling for a bit.

'Nothing—' his change of mind a ghost between us.

There is a smooth scar on his left cheek shaped like a rocket. No way of knowing how it got there. Or what happened to him. But this I reckon is what grief looks like. Filling him up. Not howling and carrying on like you see on television. Instead pooled beneath his surface, changing the shape of him.

'Tomorrow—' he says.

'Alright,' I say.

*

When I was a boy, I climbed on top of our shed roof, where I made shiny snakes with my old man's silicone gun. While I waited for the whirls to dry, I flattened myself out beneath the blue. Tracing trails left behind by aeroplanes gone.

Sky today is nothing at all, the colour has flown away. And this shed I am pushed up against is not my old man's, but instead belongs to him. He is digging in the distance, as I suck on a cigarette, my spare hand stuffed deep in my jacket pocket. He seems sad in a way that makes me want to cheer him up.

'Simon—' he calls.

I flick the dog-end into a narrow ditch that runs the length of his plot. Tread the worn line between us. He has brought me boots as we are a similar size, but they're unfamiliar. I don't feel like myself, missing my trainers. 'You alright?' I say. Up close, his eyes are hooded, hiding their colour. Today he is absent with the way he cares about me and this dirt. He has not wanted to fuck me. Chewed my lip iron raw, wondering how I have disappointed him. It could be easier to clear off.

'It's cold,' he tugs up my jacket zip all the way. The dirt beneath his nails tar black and polished. For a beat I believe he might kiss me. 'Nearly done here,' he says.

'Dunno about that,' I say. There is ground yet. Behind his head two crows swoop in the emptiness. I am reminded of my missing tower. That sting watching it fall so slow has returned, troubling me because nothing can be done. Everything eventually disappears. 'What about over there?'

'Come on,' he says.

'Alright,' I say.

*

His room smells like a memory. Smell is cunning like that. Somewhere between the bluish-green of these painted walls and my grandad's shed, is the scent of red geraniums. They flowered along his concrete yard in sunshine. Yet there are no geraniums in this bedroom, where stark bollock naked, we listen to the block of flats bang about us. Two men roar, and a dog howling move the memory away. Because grandad's geraniums are really a plastic air freshener on the windowsill, cracked open to let the cold crawl in.

'Don't know how to think about this,' he says.

The rocket on his cheek looks bright in the fading light, heading into otherness. Full of things I don't know about him. 'Me neither,' I say. Though I want to tell him something that matters. But he might think poorly of me if I confess to having never been fucked in a bed before. He gets up and pulls on his trousers. I wonder where he left my underpants all of a sudden.

In the kitchen he drinks tap water from a pint glass, watching the wall. His nipples could be bullet holes, and I want to put my palms against them. But I don't. Beside us the refrigerator hums. Taped to the white is a photograph of a girl in a blue dress. I lean in for a better look.

'My sister,' he says.

'She's pretty,' I say.

*

Four days since his geraniums that were not really flowers, and now my nostrils are ruined with piss. I am leaning behind the herd of sheds sucking on a cigarette. Blue smoke in morning light. The path here is wild with autumn. Derelict trees annoyed by ivy, and berries I don't know the name of. Behind this shed the dirt is laughing, as though it knows something of me that I have yet to figure out. Dirt is baffling.

I am not alone. Further down, a lad looks eager to mess about. He comes over, his hair makes him taller than he really is. Eyes that glint with trouble. He has a way about him, a swagger I am familiar with. I flick the dog-end away as the butt was burning my lips, and he pushes his hand down the front of my trackie bottoms. I close my eyes. Watch the sky beneath eyelids, crazy colours colliding. I am hard now without wanting to be. Because I only mean to think about *his* scar that is on its way to the moon maybe. If not for the dirt nearby taunting me, I would think I had made him up. Yesterday I went to his block of flats. Rocked on the swing in the playground beneath like an idiot, until rain moved me on.

When I open my eyes a red crisp packet flaps in the wind like an injured bird from another place. I take it as a warning, and push him away.

'Twat,' he says.

'Get lost,' I say.

*

The roof of my old man's shed was the closest I got to God. Praying more to sky than anything, because I felt less stupid. Clouds came as all kinds of creatures galloping across my view, on their way without me.

The morning after the night before, and I feel a little bit like that boy on the roof right now. Eager to be near something I can't hold on to. His breath smells of sleep, and what I reckon might be my balls. He stretches himself, says he needs the toilet. I watch his backside disappear through the door. Beside me the dent left behind is warm, but a poor fit as he is wider, and I am longer.

Dirt is how I came to be here in his bed. I don't know how the ground called, or if dirt really did. But yesterday I returned to his allotment and took it upon myself to dig what was left over. Between heavy shovelfuls I glanced up at the sky. Emptiness hung like a sheet on a line, bothering me. Then he was there. 'Simon—' he said, came and dug nearby. Close enough to persuade me I hadn't made him up.

When he returns to the bedroom, he is naked still. Stands considering me. As if he hasn't made up his mind. 'I saw you before – on the swing outside,' he says. 'Why didn't you come up?'

'Dunno,' I say. Though I decide I will tell him everything. Even my name.

He comes over and places something cool on my chest. The photograph of his sister wearing a blue dress. Sits on the side of the bed before the bare window, tells me what happened to her.

Outside the wet has settled down. Sun on the rain is everywhere.

Jon Ransom was a mentee on the 2019 Escalator Talent Development scheme at the National Centre for Writing. This year he was awarded a grant by Arts Council England to develop his creative practice. His first novel *The Whale Tattoo* will be published in spring 2022. Ransom's short stories have appeared in Foglifter Journal, SAND Journal and FIVE:2:ONE, amongst others.

A Hunger – Fran Lock

I am a fragment of my father, about whom I know nothing except for his name. My father is dead, in a tremulous and unspecified way; they speak of him in whispers if they speak of him at all. My father was named for a martyr who was named for a saint. I was named for my father. In English there are two ways to write me: with an *i* or an *e*, masculine or feminine. For most people, masculine was the default; doctors, teachers, social workers: not one of them got it right, and it never occurred to them to ask. *The affectionate form*, this is something people say about a shortened name, but they are wrong. To be littled inside of language, reduced, this is not an *affectionate* act. My own diminution was practical, not loving. People so often mistook me that my mother tired of correcting them. I have hated all my life the single syllable that remains to me: a ragged hangnail of sound, not really a *word* but a *noise*. I would mutter it under my breath sometimes, saying myself to incompletion, over again, forcing the *f*, rolling the *r*, and sensing in myself something abbreviated, sick; neither masculine nor feminine, a stutter, a mistake.

*

When I was a child, I wanted to be a boy. Not in my body, but because boys *did* things. I envied their wonderful masculine reach, their way of being in the world, the vividness of even their suffering. At home, in an atmosphere fair suffused with Irish Republican fervour, I cannot remember hearing a single song about the women prisoners in Armagh Jail. Or anywhere else for that matter. Although the blanket protests, dirty protests, and hunger strikes conducted by their male counterparts in Long Kesh were the subject of extensive lyric treatment, the women's no wash protest was never sung and barely spoken of, presumably because male shit was considered less disgusting than menstrual blood. The women in Armagh Jail were serially degraded and abused: strip-searched and sexually assaulted as a matter of policy, but the language did not exist for the specific pain of their treatment; an embarrassed silence hung over them all.

The Catholic Church had trained us for this silence. Male suffering may be exemplary, honourable, possessed of a refining fire. Men endure what is done to them, they transmute abuse into heroism. Female pain is only ever squalid, there is no dignity in *our* survival – no grace – just a grubby and stubborn persistence. When we are abused, a portion of the perpetrator's sin adheres to us. The church venerates those murdered virgin saints because survival itself is the medium of our shame, its receptacle and conduit. Men may suffer and die for a cause. Women have no cause. They suffer because they are women. This vulnerability is sordid. On the mantel, a row of dead women with the arrested pre-pubescent bodies of Olympic gymnasts; they smiled benignly as their torturers lopped and gouged at their perfect porcelain limbs.

*

My mother was fifteen when she gave birth to me. She would never say so, but in a purely objective and practical way my being born had ruined her life. I cannot remember a time when I was not aware of this, of being a tactile fragment of sin. There would be no abortion, legal or otherwise. Instead, there were desperate remedies, each more implausible and reckless than the last. It did no good, my grandmother's cunning had failed her. Whatever was me would cling to life. My mother, in turn, would cling to me. For her, I was not a source of shame or a form of punishment. I was a person. But still, the fact remains: if I had not been born, she would not have been married off to *that man*. I will not say his name. I will preserve him instead as the stifling tang of wild garlic, as a brain-dead spasm of incontinent rage. He was thick and bestial; he had thick and bestial friends. He gave us my brother. It was the single decent thing he did in the world. His family would not mix with us because we were *tinkers,* and a *tinker* is the worst sort of *taig* you can be. I do not know what he wanted with us, with her, but she was very beautiful, and he expected gratitude. Who else would touch her, want her now, *damaged goods*, with a baby in tow?

*

Aristotle says that women are merely *matter*; they cannot contribute *form* to future generations of offspring. He suggests that women are *unfinished* or *deformed.* He does not differentiate between *unfinished* and *deformed,* but uses both terms interchangeably to mean *inferior.* Tomas Aquinas states that women are *deficient* and, as it were, *unintentional*; that women are caused by weak semen or humid atmosphere, that women are both accidents and mistakes. I was not intended: my mother's misfortune, my father's mistake, doubly deformed. Because, if a woman is an accident, an accidental woman is a what?

Growing up, I understood that I was inferior for *being* a girl, but also inferior for not living up to the girl I was supposed to be. My body was an angular mass of fidgets, my hair a thicket of honey-blonde knots. I bit my nails, I rolled in the dirt. I climbed trees and frequently fell out of them. I was unequal to the dresses my grandfather brought for me. I loved their important gaudiness; their swags and ruffles and flounces, but I ruined them soon as look. All of my clothes became torn or stained. I didn't want them to. I wanted to wear the dress *and* climb the tree, but the hem would snag on a branch; I'd lose buttons and bows to a tussle with gravity or dogs. I couldn't have both. Someone was always telling me that: *you can't have both.* So I stopped wearing dresses.

I loved animals, dogs and horses especially. I had no interest in *riding* horses, I thought bits and bridles and leads were the most awful things in the world. I liked to see animals wild, living their life without reference to me. I thought wearing a collar must be like me, putting on my itchy grey school skirt, or the stiff school shoes that creaked and pinched as I walked. I liked an animal to choose me, to eat from my hand, to cooperate because they trusted or were pleased to see me. Otherwise, where's the trick? What's so special? Any fool can compel another with a big enough stick. The parents of middle-class English girls paid hundreds of pounds to seat them in a saddle and walk them on a tether, in a circle, round and round, for hours. This mystified me. Who was this for, and why? Not a relationship, a pact of dull compliance. I liked a horse running free, or to watch the boys at Ballinasloe or Rathkeevan: shirtless, bareback, bending low, about a million miles from that sawdust circle with its prissy jodhpurred somnolence, its peevish ramrod spines.

My grandfather had a tea tray, printed on which was a hologram of running horses; tilting it this way and that in my lap was an obsessive occupation. There were also lenticular prints of *The Sacred Heart of Jesus, Our Lady of Sorrows*, and best of all: wolves. I was truly obsessed with wolves; with jackals and hyenas. I was similarly bloodthirsty, accustomed to violence as both a narrative and political currency. I wanted movie-monsters, spine-chillers, slasher-flick psychopaths, Jason and Freddie. I wanted haunted dolls, possessions, dancing skeletons, talking pumpkins, ghosts and zombies, freaks and mutants. Werewolves were best of all. Disney films bored me: all those gown-bound princesses for whom *rescue* was functionally identical to *capture*. The animal characters were better, but the girls, with their damsel lashes, bore no relation to the real-life wild, where the female of the species was always bigger and stronger. Walt Disney clearly agreed with Aristotle: female animals were adapted from a standard male template with some cursory softening in strategic places. They were always pretty, delicate, symmetrical. They spoke with perfect diction. Unless they were the baddies. Or the comic relief. *Feminine* is the word I'd use, that fiendish intersection of gender and of class.

*

There are people who talk about The Gypsy Life as a vista of limitless freedoms. *Morons* is the polite term for such people. The old codes are as strict as they are exhaustive. For my grandfather's generation, and for those who came before, the world is divided into *wuzho* and *marime,* a distinction for which the body is the most immediate map: the upper body is *wuzho,* that is *pure;* the lower body is *marime,* that is or *impure* or *defiled.* Upper and lower-body clothes must be washed separately. Women's clothes must be washed separately. Spit and vomit are *wuzho,* menstrual blood is *marime.* And *marime* can't be washed away, it spreads through contact, and its contagion is both literal and moral. Things that become *marime* must be burnt, or thrown away. Where gadje hygiene seeks to cover and contain dirt, accumulating rubbish in bins within the home, for the old men, polluting dirt must be placed outside, as far away as possible. Only dirt that cannot be removed must be contained. The hem of a dress, skimming the ground. Modesty is not merely a mode of behaviour, but a spiritual condition. The *wuzho/ marime* binary proliferates a hundred thousand rules around ritual avoidance and boundary maintenance: between the upper and lower body, the inner and outer body, the inner and outer territory; between the male and the female, between ourselves and the gadje. To cross any one of these boundaries is to be hopelessly *marime.* To exist *across* is the worst thing you can do, or be. I had always understood myself as *marime.* The result and the evidence of *marime*-ness in others, but also inherently polluted and polluting for being somehow *both.* Which is to say half-blood, *poshrat,* or partial. Which is also to say not quite a girl. Which is also to say *queer.*

*

Both has a way of being *neither*. Rather, we feel this otherness in ourselves as a lack because the language we have
for it does not allow us to apprehend it as a positive quality.
Queerness is something done to the ordinary; it does not
constitute itself. It can only exist in reference to *straightness*.
It is an either-or proposition, and this is the hidden and
historical violence of *queer,* it assumes a stable centre from
which we deviate, or to which some species of deforming
damage is dealt. It has a melancholy aura, a yearning to
establish some centre of our own. What is extra in us, what
is abundant and branching and alive, feels like a hole, like
a bottomless pit into which we fall and cannot fill. That
is the cavernous quality of my own *queer* desire. Because I
can only understand myself as whole in the act of reaching
towards another, in that generous extension of affection, in
the compulsion to confirm a felt mutuality, a compassionate
commons. What I mean to say is, we talk about queerness
through desire because it is only through desire that we can
comprehend ourselves as whole, as more. Being *bi* is not,
for me, a primarily sexual proposition. Being *queer* does not
pertain to gender or sexuality alone. It is the way I am an
edge, all edge: *border-stepper, half-breed, gypo, taig,* any of the
names by which I might be known or claimed; the *marime*
part of being. *Bi* has no language, has no politics, for these
require a centre. Straight people tell me that I am *confused.*
Gay people tell me that I am *greedy,* or that I should *pick a
team,* that my love is somehow anomalous, fraudulent or
excessive. But my desire does not define or complete me,
it extends me, beyond the tyranny of *woman,* beyond the
stupid jagged fragment of my name.

*

For there are all manner of lacks and deficits in me, all manner of places I have been maimed or truncated. I have no father, and I have no *home*. When people ask me where I am from, I do not know what to tell them. I am neither English *nor* Irish. I am not Gypsy *or* Gadje. I have no *mother tongue*, no local affinities for a native territory. My accent itself is a ceaselessly shifting terrain, a rough map of halting sites and passing places; of estates and camps and squats, of transition and precarity, a relentless moving through. And I am not woman. Not in the ways I am supposed to be. At the age of thirteen my developing body became an incitement to violence, a site and occasion of trauma. And so I shaved my head and I stopped eating. This was, in the first instance, defensive: my armour against the hungry objectifying gaze of predatory men. But more than this, it was a renunciation of the world-view to which that gaze and its crass aesthetic judgements belonged. It made me, of course, another kind of target for another kind of violence. But I'd rather their ridicule than their desire; I'd rather their hate than their lust. If I cannot choose but to be abjected, I will at least choose the manner of my abjection. If I am to be torn down, I will go down swinging, denouncing that shitty, heteronormative value system and everything it wanted or expected me to be. I was already an outsider. I lived my life pulled between poles of exile and imperfect assimilation. Very well, I would own the outside. I would own my hunger, my anger. I would hone my edge.

*

A friend of mine wishes me *Happy Bi Visibility Day!* I am baffled. Talking about bi visibility feels like talking about warm snow, or dry water. *Bi* is an occulture, the visible is not its spectrum. We write and think a great deal about *bi erasure,* but supposing the opposite of erasure were not *visibility,* but *opacity?* The right to and the pleasures of the unseen; to live without the pressure to define or to perform, in the deep polymorphous silence of desire. I *would* say that, of course. A lesbian friend tells me that I am *hiding in plain sight,* inside a tedious straight marriage, benefiting all the while from an ingrained assumption of heteronormativity. And on a systemic level, of course she is right: the expectations of others form a skin of concealment. But still. I have not ceased to desire. I have not ceased in my outward or inner otherness. Each day I must negotiate my awkward fit inside this marriage, inside this straight and settled world. I am marked out by my clothes, by my decision not to have children, by my shaved head, by my unmade face, by my accent and grammar, by the depth and the difference of my cultural references, by the art I make, by the digital world I reject, by the bread I bake and the plants I grow, by the pit bull dogs I train, by the holidays I do not keep, by the saints I venerate and the incense I light, by my communism, by my veganism, by my family ties and our inherited traditions, by the way I take my coffee and tea, by the music that has sweetness and meaning to me, by the milestones of childhood experience that are alien to me, by my dislike of crowds, of parties, of people, by my contentment in my own company, my aversion to the visible, to the obvious; the inviolate privacy of my desires. It is all of this, and none of this, and more than this. Because I cannot separate my *bi* desire from everything else that I am. It is a way of meeting and being in the world, indeterminate, ambivalent, but open. And perhaps I am not a fragment of my father; perhaps my name is node, a seed. I might grow into English along either axis: masculine or feminine, *neither* or *both*.

Fran Lock is a some-time itinerant dog whisperer, the author of numerous chapbooks and seven poetry collections, most recently *Contains Mild Peril* (Out-Spoken Press, 2019) and *Raptures and Captures* (Culture Matters, 2019), the last in a trilogy of works with collage artist Steev Burgess. *Hyena! Jackal! Dog!,* a short collection of poems and essays will be released by Pamenar Press shortly, and her eighth full collection *Hyena!* is due from Poetry Bus Press later in the year. Fran is an Associate Editor at Culture Matters, and she edits the Soul Food column for *Communist Review.* Fran is a member of the new editorial advisory board for the *Journal of British and Irish Innovative Poetry.* She teaches at Poetry School. Having spent most her adult life in South London, Fran now lives in Kent.

Low Pony – Kesiena Boom

The start is a blue star of a bruise on the bone of your hip. Or rather, it's a photo of a blue star of a bruise on the bone of your hip. The photo is glowing hot on the screen of my phone. I am looking at it with scrunched-up eyes because I know what you're trying to do and I am afraid of it working. You tell me about the birth of the bruise. The hard metal pole you spin dizzily around, swooping down to the ground. I drop my phone onto the bed that I share with my girlfriend. I drop my phone face down and I squiggle my own face into a concerned spiral. I had already told you I could not go out with you. You'd asked so nakedly, entirely unafraid. 'Would you be interested in seeing each other?' The breath had caught in my throat when I'd read those words. So often I was the initiator and the feeling of being pursued gave me a thrill that felt like the exhilarating moment in a dream where you start to fall from a great height and wake up before you die. It had taken so much self-control to slowly type back 'I can't.' My girlfriend didn't want me to. Anyone but her, she'd said, when I'd told her about your proposition. And at first I listened to her.

You also had a girlfriend. Our girlfriends looked the

same. This felt relevant. When the four of us hung out, they stood together like they'd popped out of the same pod of a pea and we would stand a little apart as they talked and gaze at them in amazement, admiring how we were living a version of each others' lives. It had started so innocently.

Before you'd asked me out, the four of us had gone dancing together. You and my girlfriend were nowhere to be seen, swallowed up in the crowd by the bar. And then your girlfriend had linked her arm under mine and stroked my skin where it rose out of my dress. The dress was navy inky blue and scattered with glitter. When I moved under the lights, I gleamed like a river flashing in the sun. Your girlfriend leaned close and put her weight onto me. I felt the loop of her desire latch around me. I let the feeling run in and through me, unmoved but pleased. I had expected it, really. Because she had my girlfriend's face and my girlfriend's hair and so to my small animal brain she had my girlfriend's wants, too. In the beginning, if I was going to fuck anyone, I thought it would be her. One same-faced girlfriend switched out for another. Or sometimes, I thought it would be the four of us. Me and you and our identical girlfriends, putting our eight legs and eight arms around each other in confusing and exciting ways. No room for jealousy between our sixteen limbs. But I never thought about you and me alone. Or I didn't until you told me that you wanted me. I didn't until you started sending me blue star bruises. I didn't until I told you 'I cannot flirt with you', and you typed back quickly, 'Do what you want, but I won't stop.'

You are walking across the train platform towards my girlfriend and me. You are carrying a bag brimming with things, all spilling over. This could also be a metaphor. The last time we'd seen each other I'd let my girlfriend do most of the talking, had even been faintly jealous that the two of you had seemed to bond, that you had disappeared together into the seething sea of sweaty bodies more than once. Of course you wanted my girlfriend and not me, I thought. My girlfriend, after all, was another version of yours. It's just science, I thought. It's physics. The universe expands out and snaps back into the same place, a little bit changed, but not so much.

But between that time and now, you've been a constant buoyant bubble in my phone. I slam my thumb onto the circle of your face so many times a day I've begun to get a sharp shooting pain in the flesh of my palm. We text through school and we text through work and we text through my volunteering job where I hide in the cupboard, lifting my phone towards the heavens in order to get a better signal. We text when our girlfriends are lying next to us, turning away from their irritated faces, our focus beamed out across the narrow stretch of sea that separates our cities. You tell me about yourself and I feel a sick buzz of recognition. If you had one wish, you tell me, it would be the gift of contentment. I see myself reflected in you. The parts of me I don't always like. I look dumbly at my phone every night at 3am after we've said our goodbyes, my girlfriend slumbering beside me. The screen goes black and I am staring at myself.

On this night, as you walk down the platform towards us, I am a thread running between you and my girlfriend. I am being stretched very taut. The three of us get ready to go out together. You come close to me and admire my earrings. They are ropes of gold fashioned into the shapes of women kneeling and there are tiny pearls in the place of their breasts. I shut my eyes whilst you trace your finger around their outline. Your perfume snakes its way through my blood.

Your girlfriend messages our group chat, sad to be missing out, and tells us to have fun without her. She is away for the weekend, unknowingly spared a front row seat to what is about to go down. I pour us drinks that taste like lemons and attempt to shake off the feelings that are settling over my skin. My girlfriend looks at me periodically with warning in her eyes. I pretend not to notice. I glance at you instead, taking in the turns of your body when it is really beside me and not refracted through my phone. Did you always look like this? I ask myself. Like the shape of things to come?

The night is shifting forwards. We are at the club and my girlfriend is arguing with white girls about politics. I can see that she's overjoyed because it gives her a distraction from the oasis of need shimmering between you and me. She simmers in satisfying outrage and the white girls regard her with slack jaws. I can tell that she's trying to 'be the change' whilst simultaneously enjoying the view from her high horse. My horse is not high; I'm lolloping along on a low pony with my mind in the gutter. I grab your hand and I pull you to the bathroom. I put my face so close to yours, as close as I can get without falling off my horse. You look at me carefully. You pull away and tell me it's wrong. Your sudden moral turn only turns me on more.

We go back to dancing and I keep my eyes clenched tight. The lights are so bright I see them anyway. Impressions of orange and blue and orange again wash over me in waves. For a moment I think not of you, not of my girlfriend, but just my very own body moving methodically in space. I imagine myself tossed in the lulls of the ocean that usually separates us. I would be safer there.

The club closes and throws us back out into the night. On the train home I sit next to my girlfriend, and grasp her hand in mine. It lies motionless and damp, squeezed too hard by my sweaty, shameful fingers. She won't meet my gaze and I open my mouth silently, unsure of what to say. When we get back, the three of us wordlessly brush our teeth and wash our faces. I unclip the golden women from my ears and lie them on the counter where they look like they are praying. My girlfriend leads us both into the spare room and we huddle together on a mattress on the floor. Neutral ground. I lie in the middle. Of course.

My girlfriend is so monogamous in the warm depths of her heart. She likes the theory of moreness but the reality is far too jarring. I know she wants you too, in an abstract kind of way. I've heard her say it. She thinks you are beautiful, she understands my desire. She just cannot comprehend what I am willing to do for it. Can't fathom me mooning after you, illuminated bluely through my screen. Often we lay in bed and talked about our fantasies and hers stayed still where she left them, tucked up in the sheets. But mine unfurled and grew long legs and walked around my body and dragged me down and put their cold hands at my throat. I was always wanting. She always left me wanting.

My girlfriend is tired of our flimsy façade of platonic intimacy. She knows me too well to imagine that I'm innocent. She leans across my body, looks you in the eye and asks you what you want. When she hears the answer she pulls herself up off the mattress and tells us that we can do what we want, she cannot and will not stop us. But, if we choose the inevitable choice, then she wants nothing to do with you anymore. I watch her disappear through the door frame. A lurch of guilt/want rolls from my toes to the end of my nose. In an alternate universe we do the noble thing. But only this world exists. I think I say something dramatic like, 'It's not a real choice when there's only one option.' You look at my mouth. I am yearning for what is coming but I resist the urge to kiss you. I can wait a little longer. Until the imprint of my girlfriend's body isn't still warm beside me. I peel away and pad back to my room. I sink into bed and imagine you stretched out on the floor on the other side of the wall. My girlfriend pulls away from my touch. I don't blame her.

My girlfriend leaves before the sun is properly up. I wake to a space beside me in my bed. I know I should feel guilty but instead I cannot believe my fortune. She knows what I'm about to do and she did not try to stop me. She left. She left instead. I take this as a tacit blessing. I take liberties.

We sit and have breakfast with my housemates. Our bodies are there, clumsily eating bread and cheese with hungover hands. But our minds are already back in my bedroom, doing vulgar things to each other. We excuse ourselves from the table and slip off to the cool sheets of my bed. Later you will say it felt as natural as if we had been 'married for one hundred years.'

At first we are just lying and facing each other. You put your thigh between my legs, opening me up. I want to kiss you but I am afraid of finally getting what I want. It's been so long since I knew an unhinged desire like this. You are a storm battering against me until I am drenched and exhilarated. I put my hand in the soft of your hair. I like your severe fringe and the brown eyes peering out from beneath it. I look at your teeth, rounded and white behind the bow of your mouth. A damp feeling spreads out. You move your mouth to mine. You move your mouth everywhere. I want to cry because I'm in shock. I'm so focused on your body under/next to/over/in mine. My mind does not wander as it often does, I'm stuck fast. When I curl my fingers up into you, tears of bliss slide out of your eyes. You joke that I am killing you. Oh Jesus, please don't die, I say. You laugh and say, Jesus is alive, don't you worry. All the world shrinks down. There are no borders, only bodies. Only yours only mine only sweat only spit only more only Jesus only God only there only yes only yes only yes.

Later, I lie stupefied and you say you have to go to a birthday party, back across the sea, back in your city. Can I come with you? I ask, knowing that you will say yes. You bundle your clothes onto your body and kiss me goodbye. I will take a nap and then I will call my girlfriend. And then I will come to your house that you share with your girlfriend who is not my girlfriend and who is not me. And then we will go to the party.

My girlfriend picks up the phone immediately. She is angry and she is sad and she is resigned to the fact that I am like this. I tell her that I love her, and that my want for you doesn't diminish that. And this is true. What I don't say is that my love is ragged around the edges and has been since long before you came along. What I don't say is that she never stood a chance. What I don't say is that as soon as I put down the phone I will tumble my body underground to the train station, to be swallowed up on this side of the ocean, and spat back out on the other, at your feet.

I am in your house. Your housemate let me in. You are at the supermarket and will 'be back in five.' I go to your room and I lie on your bed. Your girlfriend's face stares down at me from the wall. I stare straight back. You appear in the doorway with your friend who will come to the party with us. I slink up against you and breathe in the soft vetiver scent of your skin. I gather you up in my arms and crush the heat of you into me. The three of us sprawl out together on the vast, hard expanse of your bed. You cut us long white lines and we disappear them up into ourselves. I'm lying on my back kicking my legs up into the air. I realise I am content. I had forgotten the feeling.

Your friend goes to the bathroom and you rush on top of me. I attempt to find some space between your atoms. I want to nestle all my fibres in between the knots of yours. I pull you hard towards me. I cannot pull hard enough. I am giddy with delight, a curious pure joy is lifting my limbs. I am so grateful for you, for drugs, for weekends, for dykes, for trains, for time stretched out.

At the party, we dance together knowing that we are beautiful. At your side I am capable of terrible things. People are staring and it turns us on. When we get home you make us a makeshift meal because we have not eaten for many hours. I open and close my mouth as if I'm reading instructions on how to do each action as I do it. It is slow work. Food seems like a sick distraction from the real work of being alive. The real work of being alive emanates from your pussy. I work my hand inside you and you cry out and tell me how good it feels. I turn my eyes to your wide open face. Our bodies are ending beginning ending beginning again. You push me onto my front, climb onto my back and fuck me whilst we look interestedly at ourselves in the mirror. I see two women who I love. They are both me, but one of them has your body.

Kesiena Boom is a dyke, writer and sociologist working across fiction, non-fiction and poetry on themes of sex, pleasure and power. She has written for *Slate* and *Autostraddle* amongst others and also writes a sex and relationships advice column.

Queer Love – Julia Bell

It's the lemon crush
you had on your teacher,
feeling thick as snow,
bending away from
rather than towards.
It's the realisation that you are
the non-conforming, non-performing,
manifestation of all the drunk variety.
It's accepting that you were born to   stand out
heads above parapets and poppies,
tall, silent, fisted, small, wrong
clothes in long rooms,
the things we should suppress
made loud, disruptive.
It's saying   *so what?*

In such a square context,
we grow in bent shapes,
our love made beautiful by our restraints.

Julia Bell is a writer and Reader in Creative Writing at Birkbeck where she is the Course Director of the MA in Creative Writing. Her work includes poetry, essays and fiction and she is published in the *Paris Review, Times Literary Supplement, The White Review, Mal Journal,* Comma Press, and recorded for the BBC. Her most recent book-length essay *Radical Attention* was published by Peninsula Press. Her memoir in verse – *Hymnal* – is forthcoming with Parthian in 2022.

Fingers in the Dirt – Sal Harris

> *My hand licks the sleep off my eyes*
> *In the middle of the garden.*
> *Sunlight and me.*
> *Fingers in the dirt reach a bone and pull it up.*
> *It's white, the most organic white. There's nothing on it.*
> *It's laid back on the ground.*
> *I'm laying down my words, suit, body, even my name.*
> *I spread it all out in front of me with the bone.*
> *To let it be seen and let it be left.*

What does transition mean?

One transition runs like water into all others. In that way, one transition is all of them.

Transition often looks like it means 'between' when actually it's the opposite of 'stagnant'. It's tempting to think that the opposite of 'stagnant' is 'moving' when actually it is so much more vast. 'Non-stagnant' can mean 'expanding'/'growing'/'developing'/'doing'/'receiving'. Any of these are transitions. Transitions are unstoppable but not always conscious.

The bone was a fox jaw.
My old name was my coat I wore every day for every hour
of my life.
Sometimes trimming the sleeves, detaching the
hood or ripping out the care label.
You can accessorise a name
and when it was alive I adorned it and altered it
in so many ways.
Couldn't leave it still, had to play with it to keep it moving.
It was the wrong name but for as long as it moved
I did not have to look at it.

What are you transitioning from/towards?

My transition has never been 'man to' anything because I was never a boy, male or man and I refuse this as my starting point. My starting point is unimportant to the concept of transition. I suppose I only know that I began with my materials and see it as my life's work to discern them, [un/re]choose them and [un/re]stitch them.

It is also unimportant where I am going since I have no end goal, only a direction.

And if it's free of a beginning and an end, isn't it guided movement? Guided living? Taking control and finding empowerment in the direction you deliberately bring energy to; like how I brought grass to the cows at the edge of the field where I grew up.

An act of love that listens to what the direction wants.

Maybe it's not about where I came from or where I'm going.
Maybe it's about what I let guide my next footprint.

> *The bone was curved.*
> *My suit was straight.*
> *It had thick shoulders that never forgave.*
> *It had fabric like silk curtains too big for the window.*
> *Big, always so big.*
> *It makes me shake to think about it.*

Why would you want to transition?

Comfort and discomfort.
The area that needs guiding is not the one you were guiding.

Of course, if you have exercised the muscles needed to guide one area of your movement for so long, then you are very good at it. Guiding the new area can be scary and unpredictable. Just by engaging in this new exercise you can learn new reasons to keep going.

> *When I put my name in the ground, when I finally left it,*
> *it didn't move.*
> *It didn't have a pulse.*
> *It was content to be left still.*
> *It even thanked me.*

> *Next to the bone I was happy to see a seedling*
> *but then only needed to look up to see that the garden*
> *was in fact already full*

> *of plants uncurling their green colours, spirits and*
> *a family of foxes.*

Why is transition magic?

It is to see a [global] spell and the choice to instead cast
your own.
It is defiant and deviant.
It is the practice of building portals specifically to enter joy.
It is radical acceptance of loss, need, desire and uncertainty.
It is the meeting of I AM, I WANT and I NEED.

If anyone tells you they fully understand transition,
know that they only fully understand their own.

The singularity of each/your transition is where we/you
reveal the/your deepest power.

Sal Harris is a queer-trans artist, writer, witch and tarot
reader. She creates work that centres intersectional feminism, eco-connection and transformative vulnerability. Her
writing focuses on queer, trans, neurodivergent and crip
politics and identities, often alongside multidimensional
connections with nature. (@sal.aitch / salaitch.square.site)

The Imaginaut – Tanaka Mhishi

I'm four when I discover that you can do a lot with a bed, a desk, a set of bedclothes and T-shirts. Some days I am a mermaid, brine slicked, emerging from the depths. Sometimes I am the sailor on the shore. Sometimes, a lion, a foundling child, a monster, a hotel chef. My mother draws me a storybook in which I am a shapeshifter. At the swimming pool I pretend I am an astronaut. I pretend that the thick silence of being underwater is actually the stillness of space. That if I reach out my hand there will be stars.

At age eight, my best friend is a girl with red-blonde hair and perfect handwriting. Her mums have the best dressing up box; it has an old blazer, a tutu, a plastic bracelet. Obviously, we get married. She looks fantastic in the blazer, and the tutu sets off my skin beautifully. Someone snaps a picture. One of her mothers officiates, and we have pasta with warm butter for our wedding feast. The floorboards of that house smell of time and energy, of linseed oil and vanilla candles and new paper. At Christmas they announce they are all moving to Australia. My friend says it like it's an adventure, but really they are being banished. Two women and a child are not yet a family in the eyes of the law. They have to leave to stay together.

We have one last meal. My father pretends to be a French waiter, and the table heaves with food. They leave to catch the start of term in January.

Age ten. Natalie and I meet in a play-by-post JRR Tolkein inspired fantasy RPG in a forum. Her character is a heroic elf warrior with flowing chestnut tresses and hazelnut, almond-shaped eyes. Frankly, she is a Ferrero Rocher. But she writes well. She describes moss and rocks so well I can almost touch them, knows how to write a fight scene. I answer with a sarcastic half-elf who utterly adores her, and we fall in love with each other's imaginations before we ever see each other's faces. She writes a paragraph. I write a paragraph. The story takes shape, and it's my first real love story. We will never meet.

Fourteen now. I am becoming good at pretending. My karate sensei is a Russian woman with stern, high cheekbones and I feel my face grow warm when she looks at me. There is a black belt boy in my class who makes me feel the same way. It's impossible to push one set of fantasies down and away without dragging the rest of them away too, so that's what I do. When my friends discuss girls they fancy, I pretend to be made of stone. I don't fancy anyone. My hair gets longer, my skin gets spottier and soon nobody even dreams that I might fall in love.

Secretly, I imagine myself the husband of the brave girl from the YA science-fiction novels I am addicted to: the girl who can shapeshift into a bear or a dolphin or a boy.

Sixteen. My body is tired of waiting. I imagine it happening in a bedroom, with the sunlight streaming in. I imagine fireworks, and the girl from my class who all the boys fancy, the one with a red streak in her hair. Instead, it's a boy. He steals two condoms from his older brother and it happens in his bathroom while the rest of our friends are having a sleepover. No fireworks, but not bad. He's kind and clever, and has a musician's hands. Soon I imagine what it might be like if we were together for a long time. I imagine that I am in love; imagine what colour I will paint our kitchen and which bit of Paris we will live in.

It lasts a year. Then he stops being kind.

At nineteen, I see a slew of dark-haired beauties of every gender. I imagine our bodies together, and sometimes it happens.

Twenty-one. I can no longer imagine. I see the plates piled high in my sink and the dirty shower water and that's it. I do not imagine having children, or falling in love, or being a writer. I do not imagine anything past the next hour. No, that's not quite true. I imagine dying. It's all I can see. I calculate the speed and weight of the trucks on the main road, the strength of a tree branch, the dosage of pills.

This is what being raped does. It obliterates the imagination.

I'm twenty-two when it begins to come back. Darker than it used to be, but still mine. Still me. I imagine my way out of the darkness. It's so hard; it's like stitching mincemeat back to life. But I do it.

Twenty-four years old now. Still, sometimes, I imagine the other life, in which I was not raped, in which I was loved better, in which my friends always stayed and the world was always kind. As the years mount up I write him letters, this me from a parallel world. He lives on a planet with no global warming, has a toddler and writes comedies.

He looks older than me, but only because he's spent more time in the sun.

Twenty-six. My best friend gets married to a bald man who looks fantastic in his blazer. She sounds like all the places she has lived: Australia, Ireland, London, America. I cry through the ceremony, then we decorate her cake together. *Imagine you, being married,* I say, and we laugh. One of her mums threatens to get out the picture of me in the tutu.

Now I am twenty-eight. My D&D group is full of queers and we are imagining our way through a vampire lord's land, and squabbling over who will get to kiss him first. I have a boyfriend who steals my socks and is kind to me. We are deciding what our bathroom might look like.

I imagine my life at thirty, and fifty and seventy-five. The heartbreak and the joy, the love and the pain and all the people I might someday be. I pretend I know now, who I am.

Sometimes, surfacing from the bath in my grown-up body, I pretend to be a mermaid. Sometimes I am the sailor on the shore.

———————————

Tanaka Mhishi is a writer and performer whose work deals with issues surrounding masculinity, trauma, sexuality and consent. He grew up in London in a mixed Sri Lankan and Zimbabwean family. His content has been produced by outlets nationwide, including BBC 3 and the Brighton Festival.

Dancing Men – Manish Chauhan

'Come on now,' the boy's mother said, bringing her rough fingers up to his face, rubbing at his wet cheeks. 'Lions don't cry.'

Now he thought of it, the boy wasn't sure whether they did or not, not that it mattered. She bent down so that their eyes were level and he saw something he didn't understand – confusion perhaps, or pity, as though she hadn't conceived of his sadness. Then all he wanted was to stop, but his hiccups kept on, and he looked down at his grazed knees, bloody from where he'd been pushed off his bike – the bike his father had given him – and he felt a fresh onslaught of tears that he knew he'd have to supress.

'We'll get you a new one,' his mother said, but Rishi didn't know who formed the 'we' in that sentence; neither of them had seen his father in a long time.

The bike was easily the most expensive of anybody at the school, with its blazing green frame, its silver spokes. It was the kind of thing Rishi imagined he'd keep forever.

'We'll need to save up,' his mother said, tightening her nightgown, turning away as she lit herself a second ciga- rette. But already he knew she wouldn't. Couldn't. And once the hiccups had eased, once he'd stuck plasters over his knees, he felt ashamed that he'd cried at all, that she'd seen him do it. He never cried. And it was clear in the way she looked at him how bemused she was by his misery. His own mother. Then he thought of the countless times he had seen *her* cry, the times he had stood behind her, put his hands over her shoulders, as if to steady her.

*

She put two of his favourite pies in the oven – an apology – mashed some potatoes and they finished a whole jug of gravy between them. Then, with his embarrassment still clinging to him, he went into his bedroom, locked the door and for the next few hours played games on his phone instead of doing his homework. At the very least, he thought, any detention would be indoors and in the warmth. Then he'd not have to worry about being chased down again, or being robbed.

He opened the window, looked all the way down their block of flats and out onto the estate. The earlier rain had washed it clean; the lights on in different blocks were reflected in shallow puddles all across the tarmac. He'd have to take the bus into school tomorrow. Or walk. Then he remembered they'd taken his wallet too, and the twenty pound note his mother had given him earlier in the week.

*

The following day, after detention, he hitched a ride on the back of Biggie's bike. They rode all the way to the park beneath the fading purple sky. It was too cold to take off their jackets, so they sat on the wet, cold grass of the hill and let their jeans grow damp. This was where they came whenever they wanted to smoke a joint and he watched as Biggie took his first, careful drag. The hill looked out onto the community centre. From where they sat, they could see straight into two of its rooms.

They didn't speak much; Biggie was one of the few people Rishi could sit quietly with, and it felt nice. Sometimes Biggie showed him porn on his phone – a girl being double-penetrated, a gangbang – and they would make bets as to which of them would be the first to try it. At other times they simply let themselves get high, quietly. Soon it would be Rishi's thirteenth birthday – then he and Biggie would be the same age, equals.

Biggie passed him the joint and Rishi took a drag, closed his eyes a little as the smoke left his mouth. He knew Biggie hadn't had sex yet, that he was waiting for Amy to dump her boyfriend so that he could ask her out – but at school they both said they had, because it was important, and because they didn't have a choice. Biggie also had a thing for Miss Reese, their P.E. teacher – he even knew where she lived.

'D'you reckon she'd let me fuck her tits?' Biggie asked, taking the joint back, pumping out small circles of smoke through his lips.

Rishi didn't say anything.

Just then he got a text from his mother.

Get us a Twix on your way back. We're out of milk.

Earlier in the day she'd sent another message telling him they'd run out of toilet paper.

From the top of the hill, the community centre looked

small, sunken into the earth, its red brick walls giving a sense of something that had only just landed, even though it had been there since before the boys were born. It opened out onto the local park where, in the summer, people went for walks and had picnics. Inside it were four rooms behind a main reception. Once, he and Biggie had seen an old woman sat naked in the middle of one of them, surrounded by artists on easels. That night Biggie had thrown stones at the window until somebody drew the curtains.

'This is good shit,' Biggie said, his head on the grass, his eyes closed, as though he were asleep, as though he were dreaming. Beneath the stillness of evening Rishi allowed his gaze to follow Biggie's profile – his thick, stubby nose; his sharp, smooth chin; his neck; the curve of his Adam's apple, all lit up by the gentle flicker of a lamppost nearby. He wanted to keep looking, but didn't.

Somewhere in the near distance they heard laughter as three men approached the entrance to the centre. The man in the middle appeared to be singing and the two on either side of him laughed. Their laughter spread itself thinly across the grass and travelled all the way up the hill. Behind those men were two more, walking in the same direction, leaning in for the occasional kiss, rucksacks pulled across their shoulders.

Biggie opened his eyes momentarily, followed Rishi's gaze, then closed them again, before passing back the joint. A light went on in one of the rooms nearest them. The men took off their jackets, their shoes and socks and put them on chairs stacked neatly against one wall. Somebody pushed open a window. A minute passed before there was music, soft music, drifting up out of the window, barely audible at first, then a little louder. It reminded Rishi of the time he and his parents had gone to Spain on holiday, a year before his father left. It was the kind of music they had played in the hotel bar at night. It made him think of an approaching wave, smooth, solid, that had yet to break.

Then somebody switched off the lights, and it took a few moments for his eyes to adjust, for Rishi to see the muted shadows of arms and legs that moved across the walls and against each other. He squinted. The men moved in circles, spinning, or stayed in one corner by themselves, moving their bodies without any rhythm, without any order, as though all that mattered was the darkness and the music. Two men danced opposite each other, like blurred reflections and Rishi looked to see whether there was somebody telling them what to do, but there wasn't.

'Fags,' said Biggie, sat up on the grass suddenly. 'Poofs.' He let out a sound – somewhere between a grunt and a laugh.

'Yeah,' said Rishi, taking his final drag and throwing the stub onto the ground. 'Twats.' Then, as though to prove it, he stood up, wiped the back of his jeans and waited for Biggie to join him, and as they rode away, he pretended not to hear the music that flowed from the window, its soft lilt full of the things he didn't want to think about.

*

'It's late,' his mother said, once he'd put toilet roll, milk and a Twix on the kitchen counter. 'Where were you?'

'With Biggie,' he said.

'His name's Gurminder!' she said. 'Why doesn't anybody call him by his proper name?'

He opened the fridge to put the milk in.

'How was school?' she asked, which surprised him, because she never asked, but by the time he had thought of something to tell her, she was already back on the sofa, turning the volume up on the television, biting into her Twix.

He had a quick shower to gid rid of the smell, then came out and sat beside her. She spent all day working, left to clean the factories long before he was up in the morning. The evenings were all they had, and if ever he was late home he knew it would take some time for her to talk to him properly, to forgive him.

Some time passed before he felt her body slacken against his, felt the press of her shoulder.

'How much do you reckon a new bike would cost?' she asked.

'About four hundred,' he said.

She let out a sharp breath.

'It'll take a while to save that much.'

'It doesn't matter,' he said, even though it did.

He seldom saw his father but last year, on Rishi's birthday, he had driven all the way from London to give him his bike. He'd taken him out for lunch too, although they didn't have much to say. And there had been a moment, just before his father drove off, and with the bike stood solid beside him, that Rishi understood that it might be a very long time before they saw each other again. Seeing the bike in the hallway, morning after morning had granted him a kind of relief, as though it were proof of the life they'd once lived.

Now in its place was nothing.

He thought of whoever had taken it, imagined them riding it at full speed down the main road. The bike that was his.

'Oh Rish, I bought something,' his mother said, reaching for a bag by the side of the sofa. She pulled out a red dress with white flowers painted over it. He watched as she stood up and dangled it in front of herself.

'It looks nice,' he said, even though he thought the red too bright – the kind of red that would need her to wear make-up. But she was smiling, the soft material swaying gently around her hips.

'You're such a good boy,' she said, bringing her hand to his cheek before she folded the dress and put it neatly back into the bag. 'You always take good care of me.'

He didn't know what to say.

'You know how to treat people. Unlike your father.' She sat back down. 'When you get yourself a girlfriend, you'll treat her properly, I already know it. You'll make such a good boyfriend.'

He felt himself grow hot.

She sighed and closed her eyes. 'You'll marry a lovely girl,' she said, and you'll get a good job, and you'll have a nice big house like the one we used to live in, and you'll have children of your own and it'll all work out Rish – you just wait.'

After dinner he left her watching a film in the lounge. Still warm from the weed, he went to his room and thought about the things she had said, each one heavy, like rocks in his pocket. Slowly his high diminished.

He locked the door, pulled out his phone and read Biggie's latest text. Once he'd clicked on the link, he watched two girls fuck each other using strap-ons. He tugged at himself. Nothing. Then he closed his eyes and thought of Biggie instead. Biggie watching the same clip, getting himself off until he came, hard. Rishi felt himself stiffen. And once he'd finished, he waited for the euphoria to make its way steadily across his body, to ease him into sleep, even though it wouldn't. Instead, his head filled with thoughts of the men at the community centre, dancing their stupid little dance without a care in the world. He felt embarrassed, then angry, livid almost, although he couldn't say why.

*

A week later he and Biggie rode back up the hill. Earlier in the day, it had snowed. The ground was frozen, solid. Their joint was the only thing that offered up any warmth. Biggie took off his jacket, lay himself on the grass then pulled the jacket up to cover himself. He moved his shoulders up and down, made himself comfortable.

'We should try a bong one day,' he said. 'It's more intense.'

Rishi lay down too, until they were beside each other. It felt good, just the two of them and from the corner of his eye, he watched as Biggie closed his. He hadn't seen anybody look so comfortable, as though nothing else mattered. He wanted to look away but couldn't. Then, without giving it too much thought, he moved closer, looked at Biggie's lips and wondered what would happen if he kissed them. He moved even closer, until their mouths were centimetres apart but before anything more could happen, Biggie opened his eyes.

'What the fuck,' he said, shuffling away, as though he'd seen a rat.

Rishi moved back, lay his head on the grass.

'I ain't a fag,' Biggie said. 'No way.'

'Fuck you. I wasn't trying anything. I thought I could see something on your face.'

'Like what?'

'A spider or something.'

But the spell had been broken, and before long Biggie said he had to go. Rishi watched him disappear down the hill, the lights on his bike growing smaller and smaller until they were nothing.

Now alone, he wiped his wet eyes with the back of his hands.

Beneath the black fog, he heard the soft familiar-unfamiliar music float up out of the centre and knew exactly what it was. He watched the men, their shoulders, their calves twitching in the half-light. Their blurry shadows moving gently across the wall, their hands sometimes clasped, sometimes free, like birds traversing the sky. It made him feel sick.

'Stupid fucking fags,' he shouted as he stood up and walked towards the main road.

*

It would be another twenty minutes before he returned, the cold having numbed him, his nose red, running. He pulled two empty bottles out of his rucksack that he'd bought at the local shop, a litre of alcohol, some dry dish cloths.

Once the bombs were ready, he used the lighter Biggie had forgotten to take off him, and as two flaming bottles flew through the air and smashed the windows, he felt a rush at how successfully they'd met their target, at the sheer force with which they landed, and as soon as he saw the orange flicker burst through the room, he ran down the hill and hid amongst some trees.

Through the leaves, he watched the furious plumes of fire and smoke that were his creation, that devoured the inside of the community centre. The thrill of it lit up his insides, made him smile, then laugh. He felt the blood race through his body. An alarm went off but still the flames whirled higher and higher, screamed louder and louder until Rishi wondered how much longer it would take for the whole thing to burn to the ground.

*

He walked home slowly, told his mother he wasn't hungry, but he was so late that she didn't look at him. He told her he was tired and going to bed, and she waved her hand to show that she had heard.

In his room he lay on the bed and stared up at the ceiling. He thought of the raging fire, the smoke, the frantic men, the wailing siren, then closed his eyes and tried to think of nothing, but the flames had already found their way beneath his eyelids, etched themselves onto his brain so that they were all he could see. He thought of the men who'd have nowhere left to dance, then he pulled his quilt up to cover his face, in the hope that it would smother everything in darkness. But it wouldn't, and before long he heard the soft, familiar-unfamiliar music ringing about his ears, threatening to fill them up.

Manish Chauhan is British-Indian, studied creative writing at the University of Oxford and is an alumnus of Curtis Brown Creative. He came second in the Exeter Story

Award and Evesham Festival of words and was shortlisted for the Curtis Brown First Novel Prize and the DGA First Novel Award.

Sympathy for the Villain: A Queer Memoir of Online Video Game Fandom – Kathryn Hemmann

It's no secret that many villains are coded as queer. Consider the terrible wizard, resplendent in his fine robes at the top of his tall and phallic tower, or the evil queen, with sharp cheekbones and even sharper eyes, gazing into the depths of her yonic mirror. There is the vampire who emerges from his closed coffin at night to satiate an unspeakable desire, and the werewolf who shifts from one form to another with the phases of the moon. Is it any wonder that so many queer people sympathize with monsters?

Mainstream pop culture has no shortage of fabulously over-the-top villains, even in stories ostensibly intended for children. There is the devious usurper Scar in *The Lion King*, catty and intellectual in the face the stolid patriarch-king and his many wives, or the slinky and seductive sea witch Ursula in *The Little Mermaid*, modeled on the legendary American drag queen Divine. For better or worse, even *Harry Potter* didn't miss a beat in coding its main villains as gay, from two men magically sharing the same body in the first novel to two men magically locked in a fatalistic failed romance in the prequel movies. When a group of *Harry Potter* fans on social media attracted mainstream attention by reading the caustic potions master Severus Snape as a transwoman, they were celebrated in online news outlets for reclaiming the queer coding that was already readily apparent within the text.

There is something about queerness that reads as devious and upsetting to people who live the majority of their lives in normative society. To some of us, however, that very strangeness serves as the appeal of queer characters, villainous or otherwise. How delightful it is to encounter a fictional character who looks and talks like you but vehemently refuses to be boring. Villains are confident and proud, and they clearly aren't afraid to be disruptive. As an added bonus, villains are often fascinating and unique. Any kid with a sword can become a hero, but it takes a special type of person to become the final boss.

In a perfect world, queer people could express our identities in all aspects of our lives, but the real world isn't so simple. Even as many societies have become steadily more progressive, queer identities and sexualities are still considered transgressive. It can be extraordinarily difficult to navigate the world as a queer person, especially when something as mundane as using the bathroom or simply washing your hands can feel like stepping onto a battlefield. For the sake of our own survival, we learn to keep our heads down and follow the rules that dictate what it means to be normal. Pride is fantastic, but someone still needs to pay the rent.

Fantasies are important to queer people, both as a means of dealing with the frustrations of daily life and as a way to imagine what a different world might look like, and video games are a key medium for fantasies of queerness. Even if a game doesn't allow you to customize your character and pursue the relationship of your dreams, many games allow the player a degree of direct agency that isn't present in other forms of entertainment media. There's no need for anyone, queer or otherwise, to play any given game 'straight,' with modding and speedrunning communities breaking down and redefining how a game is 'meant' to be played and what story it tells. As gaming scholar Bonnie Ruberg has argued, video games have always been queer.

The contemporary medium of video games has grown up alongside social media, and game designers and journalists such as Anna Anthropy and Leigh Alexander have chronicled the explosive formation of queer-friendly gaming communities in online networks and venues. Some of these communities express queerness through the celebration of imagined relationships between characters in fanfiction and fancomics, while some queer fandoms revolve around antiheroes and outright villains, from the cartoonish Bowser of the *Super Mario* games to the sinister Queen Nashandra of the *Dark Souls* franchise. The appeal of an impossibly strong and gleefully subversive character who can't be defeated until the very last second is undeniable, and the queer subtext of such villains is often brought to the forefront by fans who incorporate these characters into their shared fantasies and online rituals of identity formation.

Fandom is a beautiful thing – or rather, fandom can feel that way until you get your first anonymous message urging you to schedule a lobotomy or informing you that, if you're a fan of a certain character, then you are *literally* Hitler.

The internet has never been a safe space. When anyone can say anything, someone inevitably will. Nevertheless, the #Gamergate campaign of targeted harassment directed at young women during the summer of 2014 marked a horrifying moment not just in the visibility of online violence, but in its intensity as well. The online message boards that generated festering resentment against female game developers and gaming journalists also incubated the rise of the political movement now referred to as the alt-right, which played a key role in the 2016 American presidential election, as well as elections (and resistance against elections) in Europe.

The rise of the alt-right is complicated, especially in an international context. What was perhaps less complicated was the backlash from progressive communities, especially in the online spaces that provided homes for young creators to post their fanwork, the fannish social network Tumblr first among them. In response to the harassment campaigns of the alt-right, community leaders in progressive communities doubled down on their own rhetorical aggression. The language of political and cultural feminism was weaponized, with terms such as 'abuse' and 'pedophilia' being used to describe anyone whose interest in fictional characters was perceived to be politically or ideologically impure.

The intensity of such discourse on Tumblr became so pervasive that, at the end of 2017, the site was compelled to change its terms of service to state that adult content would be deleted from the site, presumably after the app was removed from Apple's App Store after being flagged as a conduit for 'abuse' and 'pedophilia.' In the end, the people who ended up being the most affected by Tumblr's new policy were young people with queer sexualities who had found a haven in the site's relaxed and progressive atmosphere. Ironically, although fictional characters can't be hurt, real people most certainly can, and the most vulnerable people on the platform had the most to lose.

None of this was new to those of us who have always felt sympathy for the villains. A group of 'heroes' adamantly insists on misunderstanding you and treating you as an abstract concept while refusing to listen to you as a person. Queerness, in its refusal to conform to normative social standards, has a long history of being interpreted as 'evil' and somehow 'harming the children.' To be queer is to receive constant social messages that you're at fault for existing as yourself in public, after all.

Self-confidence is easier said than done, so what happens when you're treated as a monster even by other monsters? Many people in queer online communities have found solidarity in their outsider status, but many others have lost the only community they had because they weren't queer in a way that was considered to be trendy or socially acceptable. Community rejection stings even more fiercely than broad social discrimination, especially when it's tied to personal hobbies and creative expression. It goes without saying that online harassment can have severe effects on a person's wellbeing, no matter which end of the political spectrum is sending anonymous hate messages.

Well-intentioned people might advise members of the digital generations to just log out, but such an extreme response isn't a viable solution. A creative person who shares their work online may as well be told not to create, or not to exist at all. In the end, that's what 'just log out' advice amounts to: a reminder that existing as a queer person is bad and harmful, even to your own self. The message seems to be that the fault lies not in the prevailing social atmosphere that facilitates and excuses harassment, but rather in *you* for being so, you know … queer.

Is it any wonder so many villains are coded as queer, then? And is it any wonder that so many queer people love and sympathize with villains? Without the sort of difference of identity and perspective that results in conflict when it challenges the status quo, how interesting can a game or story be? If the status quo insists on treating you as a villain, why *not* destroy the world?

The anger of villains is real, and there is power in anger. There is power in solidarity too, and strength in banding together with a brave party of fellow adventurers to form a supportive community. Perhaps, however, it's not always the villain who needs to be defeated at the end of the game. After all, the best type of story is when the heroes learn to see their world from a different perspective.

References

Alexander, Leigh. *Breathing Machine: A Memoir of Computers.* New York: Thought Catalog, 2014.

Anthropy, Anna. *Rise of the Videogame Zinesters: How Freaks, Normals, Amateurs, Artists, Dreamers, Drop-outs, Queers, Housewives, and People Like You Are Taking Back an Art Form.* New York: Seven Stories Press, 2012.

Lees, Matt. 'What Gamergate should have taught us about the "alt-right."' *The Guardian,* 1 December 2016. https://www.theguardian.com/technology/2016/dec/01/gamergate-alt-right-hate-trump

Ruberg, Bonnie. *Video Games Have Always Been Queer.* New York: NYU Press, 2019.

Stephen, Bijan. 'Tumblr's porn ban could be its down-fall — after all, it happened to LiveJournal.' *The Verge*, 6 December 2018. https://www.theverge.com/2018/12/6/18127869/tumblr-livejournal-porn-ban-strikethrough

Tourjée, Diana. 'The Shockingly Convincing Argument That Severus Snape Is Transgender.' *Vice*, 29 June 2017. https://www.vice.com/en/article/bjx8xm/the-shockingly-convincing-argument-that-severus-snape-is-transgender

---

Kathryn Hemmann is a Lecturer and Research Associate at the Center for East Asian Studies at the University of Pennsylvania, where they study contemporary Japanese fiction and video games. Their book *Manga Cultures and the Female Gaze* advocates for the practice of looking at popular entertainment media from a queer perspective.

It Starts with Names
Spat – Dale Booton

at the body liquid
chastising of its limpness   its seemingly lacking
interest in the physicality of how it should behave
so it is told   again and again and again   the way a
record scratched to fuck cannot help but hear itself
jitter the only two notes it can reach   like a cry for
help   over the years the body will bleed its tears
into the night   clutching its pillow like a wounded
friend   the two of them watching as the sky bids
farewell   turns its back   then the body will try to
distract comfort with a ruler to the genitals   will
try to beat the self into submission   will tear itself
from itself in the hope that the sacrifice will offer
surrender   that getting too close to the knife will
just be a pitstop on the road to becoming beautiful

Dale Booton is a twenty-six-year-old queer poet from Birmingham. His poetry has been published by Verve in their Diversity anthology and The Young Poets Network. Most recently, his poetry has been featured by *Ligeia*, *Queerlings*, *Fahmidan*, Tealight Press, *Spelt*, *Dreich*, and *The Adriatic*. He is currently working on his first pamphlet.

The Girl I Left Behind
Me – Honor Gavin

It is just gone quarter past six by the time she leaves the office. By saying 'she' I'm already taking liberties, because the only pronoun used for the protagonist of the story *in* the story, the title of which is also my title, is 'I'. In Muriel Spark's 'The Girl I Left Behind Me', the nameless first person protagonist is gendered only by her implied identification with the eponymous 'girl' 'left behind', by her relation to a particular genre of femininity – worrying – and by her fate: violent death at the hands of the man she works for, whose name is – funnily enough, given she's his secretary – Mark Letter. We learn of this fate at the very end of the story, at the same time that she does, when she returns to the office having gone home on the bus but having not been able to stop thinking that she has forgotten something. 'Perhaps I had left the safe unlocked, or perhaps it was something quite trivial which nagged at me,' she thinks. The story, then, has three ways of ending, each of them twisted: with the scene of her murder, with the realisation that the narrating 'I' worrying her way home from work and back again has been, all this time, her own ghost, and with the unexpected manner in which the unliving protagonist meets her lifeless body. 'With a great joy I recognised what it was I had left behind me [. . .]. I ran towards my body and embraced it like a lover'.* At this point, the sadness that has dappled her thoughts throughout the story finally lifts.

It is, I'll admit, somewhat troubling to suggest, as I have done, that worrying is gendered, or that femininity has a particular relation to it, or that worrying as a *genre* – toned as it is by 'misty unease' and triviality – is on a par with violent death when it comes to considering the ways in which identities might be said to be marked. But the story's point is powerfully clear. The protagonist's gender is fatal in the sense that it propels her towards an otherwise motiveless death – we're given no other reason for the murder – and yet this gender is never named explicitly but only surfaces in negativity, in the everydayness of her erasure, the grinding mundanity of her lack of presence – 'No one at the bus stop took any notice of me. Well of course, why should they?' – and her fretting about forgetting something or leaving something incomplete. Her humdrum worrying is not out of sync with her unfair fate, this suggests, but structurally intimate with it, even a symptom of it. Her trivial worries and unextraordinary weariness are the flipside – the index or register – of the way in which her existence is adumbrated by a kind of deathliness. No wonder, then, that she loves her own loss. Why shouldn't she? The story's surprise ending is also a moment of agency. For once she's not worrying. She wants something: a body no longer 'hers'.

---

* All references are to Muriel Spark, 'The Girl I left Behind Me' (1957), in Muriel Spark, *The Complete Short Stories* (Edinburgh: Canongate, 2018), pp. 278–283.

*

To over-identify with something is to associate yourself with it excessively, maybe perversely. It's a form of identification that misrecognises whatever it is that is being identified with at the same time as it seeks out a special closeness or intimacy. It sees a promise in the object that the object does not necessarily hold. I'm not usually very interested in whether or not I identify with somebody or something in fiction – reading fiction for me has always been a way of experiencing vicariously, of taking leave of what I already know – but now, in relation to Spark's 'The Girl I Left Behind Me', I find myself wanting to over-identify. I want to read the story in such a way that refuses its fatalism while also embracing its arresting eroticism, and I want to misrecognise it – read it excessively, maybe perversely – in terms of a story it doesn't hold: my own.

I'm not a girl, but I've been taken for one. I've occasionally named myself as one. Despite the slight misogyny of the word when used in relation to a fully-grown adult, I've sometimes preferred the category of 'girl' to that of 'woman', perhaps exactly because 'girl' is slighter, less present, less consequential. Easier to shrug off. I'm not a girl and I never was, but it has taken me a long time to say so directly, as opposed to obliquely, under a wash of negativity, and only now, in my mid-thirties, am I starting on the hormones that are beginning to return my body more fully to the boyishness of its earlier years. Only now I am beginning to recognise myself in my body's contours, as opposed to deferring – not completely acquiescing, but something close to it – to others' ways of taking and naming me. In Spark's story, I notice, 'The Girl I Left Behind Me' is not only the story's title but the name of a song hummed by the man the so-called 'girl' works for, Mark Letter, also her murderer. The song worms its way into the protagonist's head too: 'Teedle-um-tum-tum,' she hums as her bus lurches. In the story, the 'girl' is only named as such by the song she has heard the man she works for humming. Likewise, the feeling of fussiness she experiences during the workday – 'I felt fussy for the rest of the day', she tells us – has its origins in Mark Letter's 'moods of bustle', to which she is expected, endlessly, to attend.

No wonder Spark's protagonist is delighted to be done working for him, and delighted, too, to see 'herself' done with. But something I am also noticing is this. Only in leaving her behind me – only in the moment of saying goodbye to her – am I willing to let this girl who never was live a little. Just a bit. Only in the moment of no longer being beholden to her body am I willing to embrace her, even take a little of her with me – in the form of a femininity I can delight in from the distance of my increasingly visible masculinity, rather than feel buried by – into whatever comes next.

*

Why is this? Why do I find myself feeling a tenderness for a femininity I've hated – despised wearing and felt so worn down by – up until this point? Why did it take me so long to get back to where I left off? Why does the protagonist of Spark's story return to her lifeless body like a lover might and what is the name of her pleasure in that moment? Masturbatory? Necrophiliac? There are problems, of course, in eroticising death when gratuitous excessive death of the kind Spark's protagonist meets with is something some identities are marked out for more so than others – but nonetheless, the protagonist of Spark's story ends up embracing the body that is no longer tethered to 'her'. What might I make of this moment given my desire to over-read it? Is there a residue – a remainder – of lesbianism here?

'Lesbian' was the word I reckoned with when, eventually, I came into my queerness the first time around. Not because that was what I was – I always felt an unaccountable distance to the category even as my life collided with it – but because of the style of an earlier encounter. 'Lesbian' was the word I had heard in my head over and over when, aged about thirteen or so, I became sure it was the word the girls at school were using for me behind my back – the broken song being hummed about me, 'teedle-um-tum-tum'. That certainty was also the birth of my paranoia, a paranoia that still lurks in my daily life and a paranoia born in deadlock, because what I was paranoid about in that early moment was not something completely unfounded, but truthlike – an approximation, a nearness if not a naming. It took me years to actually get there, but when I did, when I left behind another life, hardly lifelike, it was via the word I'd been called in my head over and over again back then. The word 'lesbian' therefore simultaneously marks my acknowledgement of my queerness and the beginnings of the mental distress – an unrelenting and often excruciating hypervigilance – that has remained with me since. 'Paranoia' is and is not the right word for it. 'Paranoia' names the pattern of the thinking, but paranoia is supposed to be what happens when the held suspicion has no supporting evidence in the real world – but in my case, in that early encounter with the word 'lesbian', the paranoia *was* the evidence. That was the painfulness. That was what 'lesbian' named, I guess – my distance and proximity to my queerness.

But for these very reasons, I will always have a fondness for it. A softness for it. A way of folding myself into the word even while my body and mind have taken leave of its signification – of its meaning. It is where I have lived things out, even if it is not quite the right word for the kind of living I have been doing.

*

What's the relationship between worrying and paranoia? In 'The Girl I Left Behind Me', the difference is difficult to locate, exactly because the protagonist's bus-journey worries about insignificance and inexistence – though they seem to attach to silly little nothings like her bus ticket not being checked – turn out to be grounded in truth. 'I thought how nearly no one at all I was', she says, and in the end she's correct. The story's conclusion retroactively translates the protagonist's worries into a paranoia that is no paranoia at all.

I've spoken of that early moment of hearing the word 'lesbian' over and over, a slur said of me in my head, as the beginnings of my paranoia. That's true but it's also an equivocation, because what it doesn't explain is my susceptibility to paranoid thinking, my tendency to think that way, the switch that was flicked. Susceptibility is a way of naming our relation to something we may come to be, but not necessarily; it's a kind of fate, but one we might avoid. Or else make work for us in unexpected ways. What made me susceptible to paranoid thinking was, I think, precisely my femininity – itself in some ways a kind of susceptibility – which I wasn't born with but which came at me violently. I was feminized by an earlier violence or violation – it's happened to many – and as the years passed I often felt my femininity as a form of attrition or a slow kind of dying. I am not saying that that is what femininity necessarily is – I'm saying I couldn't feel it as anything but secretarial, a servicing, and I felt too a resentment of the expectation that I might have anything in common with others who happened to be marked by it. The pressure to identify with those with whom I was presumed to share a gender never felt very promising to me. But to be clear, the earlier violence I am talking about was not the cause of my transness, but the cause of my femininity, which in my case was – and again, I am not by any means saying that it *always* is – caught up in a constant worrying, a fretting that kept collapsing into paranoia. It wasn't mine, my femininity, but I was left with it, and now that I'm leaving it, I am able to make a kind of peace with it.

This is also, I guess, my answer to the question of the connection between worrying and paranoia. Worrying by and large attaches to actual problems – often tiny, often lots of them simultaneously. It's for this reason that worrying feels domestic wherever it takes place, be it the office or workplace; it is orientated towards care-giving. Worrying over-notices – that's where its atmosphere of 'misty unease' comes from. Paranoia doesn't care whether its problem is real or not – it doesn't notice. It is for this reason perhaps more masculine. Thinking about it, maybe I have paranoia to thank for helping me to stop worrying.

*

In any case, it is just gone quarter past six.

Honor Gavin is a queer transmasculine writer from Birmingham. *Midland: A Novel Out of Time* (Penned in the Margins in 2014) was shortlisted for the Gordon Burn Prize. Their short story, 'Home Death', was longlisted for the Galley Beggar Press Short Story Prize. They currently live and work in Manchester, UK.

The Glass Hammer – Leon Craig

M

By the Valentine's Day of that year, Rosie had tried to break up with Maya at least twice, but Maya wasn't having any of it. She would be making mussels in a white wine sauce with hand-cut chips, creamed spinach and macaroons to follow. The green amber earrings that Maya would insist matched Rosie's eyes had lain wrapped in pale blue tissue for months. Maya had tried to buy them in secret during their holiday in Prague, but Rosie had complained she was cold waiting outside the shop. Maya relented and told Rosie to go look at the huge display of Bohemian garnets. She was pretty sure Rosie knew what she was getting. Maya had decided she was too sallow to wear the amber herself and tried to feel pleased that she'd talked Rosie out of leaving her.

R

Rosie did not remember any particular eloquence, but rather the fear that Maya might do something drastic. She hadn't thought it was possible for anyone to cry so much. Maya cried at books and plays, and when she couldn't understand maps, which was pretty much whenever she tried to use one. She cried when she was stressed or overwhelmed, but often she cried for no reason at all.

'How can you just be sad for no reason? Something must have set you off.'

'There honestly isn't a reason. Can't we talk about something else instead?'

After they had said they loved one another, Maya told her she'd cried on and off for a week after she'd realised. This was supposed to be romantic. The way she cried creeped Rosie out. Other people scrunched their foreheads up or sobbed or went pink in the face, but often Maya would cry motionlessly, as if her eyes had become independent from her face. When they were out together, Maya behaved herself and seemed like the cheerful, confident person Rosie had originally pursued. Rosie had once come round to find Maya lying fully dressed for a party with a camomile teabag over each eye, hoping to conceal how she had spent that afternoon.

'Your friends won't care you're sad, they're your friends.'

'They will care, at least four of them will be delighted.'

'Sounds like they're shit friends, you should get new ones.'

'Friendship is complicated, you must know that.'

'No, we just shout at each other and then it all blows over in a few days. We need each other too much to hold grudges.'

M

Valentine's Day was also their anniversary. Maya hated Valentine's Day and had established a yearly tradition of anti-romantic gestures, the highlights of which included getting both nipples pierced, going on a solo tour of Highgate Cemetery and getting so drunk on cachaça that she'd had to be carried home. The year before this one, she had gone to the Muddler in Dalston with the intention of waking up next to someone unsuitable and woken up next to Rosie. Her attempt to explain that she couldn't have a relationship had not been well received, though they did continue sleeping together. Neither of them were entirely certain when they had become girlfriend and girlfriend so they decided to count from Valentine's Day.

R

Rosie had admired Maya a great deal. Her unfamiliarity with a lot of popular culture seemed charming, like she'd stepped out of another era. Rosie hadn't yet experienced the particular hell of trying to get someone who has a lot of opinions on Bergman to sit down and watch Family Guy at the end of a long day without providing a running socio-political commentary on Peter's antics. All the things Maya liked were sad and complicated and two hours long with subtitles. She didn't seem to believe in enjoyment and was quietly but perceptibly hostile to the many of the things Rosie enjoyed. The only time she wasn't asking annoying questions or trying to start an argument was when they were having sex.

M

Maya found she enjoyed being swaddled in sleep-smelling sheets, with Rosie's ponytail tickling her neck. After years of insomnia, she rediscovered the simple pleasure of drifting in and out of consciousness. But she was distressed that there were so many hours when they were awake that could not be filled with body. Was she supposed to talk for all of those? Was Rosie? She missed having those hours to herself, though she had wasted enough of them staring at the ceiling and wishing either for the resolution to end her life or to put the question aside for good.

R

Rosie had initially been sympathetic, when she thought Maya was just having a bad couple of weeks.

'It's OK. You can talk to me. I've gone through some difficult times too.'

'Thanks, but it's always been like this, so there's no point.'

'But if you're sad, that makes me sad too. I want to help you.'

'When it gets too much for you, just go into another room for a bit and read a book while you wait for me to calm down. There isn't anything you can do except ignore it. It's very uninteresting.'

'Isn't there someone at uni you could talk to about getting therapy?'

'I've had therapy. I don't see the point in having more, you would just expect me to get better. Don't engage with it as a narrative.'

'You're not a story, Maya, you're my girlfriend.'

M

'You say that like those things are contradictions.'

R

Rosie remembered that Maya had once told her about the secret language of carnies. She had been researching an essay and read somewhere that most groups develop their own micro-dialect. This was particularly true for tight-knit groups who are apart from society for one reason or another. There could even be a private dialect within families or between two people, which nobody else understood quite as well if it wasn't intended for them. American carnies had a whole range of words and phrases and even jokes known only to one another. On joining the fair, an unwary initiate would be sent up and down the site, getting more and more frustrated in search of some mythical but useless item, like a glass hammer. Rosie didn't understand how anyone could fall for something so obvious.

M

Not long before they were officially together, there had been an evening on which Rosie tried and failed to engage Maya in conversation on Messenger. Initially, Maya had been friendly, even flirtatious, but then let the pauses between her replies grow longer and longer. Rosie started asking her yes/no questions, thinking that might prompt her to respond. After Maya had been quiet for forty minutes, she lost her patience and asked, 'Why are you ignoring me?' Maya eventually replied that she was trying to write a story and was too busy to talk.

R

Rosie decided she must be lying to get rid of her. Had she been with someone else? Months later, Rosie decided to ask.

'I really was writing a story. My phone kept distracting me, so I put it face down and didn't see your messages.'

'Can I read it?

'No, it's not good enough.'

91

'You're just saying that. I want to read it anyway.'

'It's too metaphysical. I'm better when I'm writing about people and relationships.'

'Have you ever written about me?'

'No. It would hurt your feelings.'

'So you want to say loads of mean stuff about me? That makes me feel great, thanks.'

'Nobody is all good or all bad. If I wrote about you, I couldn't just praise you, that would be boring, even if it were the truth.'

'So the fact you love me is boring? Why don't you understand that lying isn't OK? Everyone else gets taught that as a child.'

'Conversation is as much an art as anything else. And besides, all good lies need a little truth in them to be believable.'

'If you ever write about me, I'm going to go back to Prague and smash our lock.'

M

They hadn't thought to call ahead, reasoning that the Czech Republic had approved civil partnerships years before Britain. But the girl at the desk asked Maya to repeat herself, and then started muttering in Czech on the phone, very obviously about them. The love lock bridge was corny, but it felt novel to show affection in public, with other couples, and not have to hear anyone's opinion about it. Maya couldn't recall a single other display of affection which a man had not interrupted in some way, from cheering, to telling her that Jesus didn't die so she could do this, to informing her that it turned him on. Once, while she was walking Rosie home through the dark, a man had followed them in his car for several streets, shouting out of the window 'two hundred pounds for some cock', as if he would be paying them to take it away. Maya liked to finish the anecdote with 'which gives a whole new meaning to fly tipping.' Actually, she had walked the whole way home arranging and rearranging her keys between her knuckles, ready to hook his eyeball out if he tried anything.

R

At times Rosie thought things were getting easier. But then she would hear Maya reshaping anecdotes so that they sounded better, or see her wincing every time Rosie mixed up 'bought' and 'brought', even though she knew that Rosie knew they meant different things.

'Why does it matter? Why do you have to be such a control freak about language?'

'Because it's the most important thing. It's the only thing. All that remains of us is what has been recorded. Speaking and writing determine what exists and what keeps existing.'

'Um, no. What exists determines that.' She hated when Maya tried to make their issues as a couple into philosophical debates.

'But lots of things only exist because people talk about them ... Most relationships only exist in language. Otherwise it's just two people sleeping together.'

Rosie tried to not to rise to that one.

'We had to agree on that, though. You can't just decide the truth and say it by yourself.'

'I can if there are no other extant accounts. Or if my version is the most compelling.'

M

Maya was frequently amazed by Rosie's inability to endure things. Inclement weather, tension, any sort of physical discomfort provoked an immediate reaction. There seemed to be no gap between registering a sensation and agitating to fix it. 'I'm starving.'

'It's five thirty. I'm still writing my coursework and I can't start cooking supper until eight. I'll make you a snack, if you want one.'

'But I want us to eat together.'

'We can do that later.'

'Why don't we just go to mine? There'll be enough food for you too.'

'Your mother hates me, she thinks I made you gay.'

'No, you hate her because she doesn't read.'

R

Damien breathed through his mouth, very loudly. It was almost like panting. Rosie's desk was angled so her monitor could be seen by the rest of the office, including the eternally inquisitive Damien. Mostly, she entered data from the feedback forms onto spreadsheets. Often, there were long periods where not much happened at all. Rosie tried to look at pictures of cats and baby platypuses and bunnies. If she thought about them hard enough, she could almost feel their fluff under her hands and feel their tickly whiskers brushing her wrists. For added realism, she imagined a slight smell of sawdust. Damien said that if she kept using the office computer to look at pet pictures, she would get an official warning. When she told Maya this, Maya asked why she couldn't read poetry instead, since she was going to start her degree soon.

M

Maya had been taught that silence was a way to avoid acknowledging unpleasantness, but Rosie used silence as tool to make it known.

'So, how was work today?'

[silence]

'Did anything interesting happen?'

[silence]

'I found some great articles about Burton and scholar's melancholy. Did you know Charles VI had iron rods sewn into his clothes because he thought he'd shatter if someone touched him?'

[silence]

'You're ignoring me, aren't you?'

[silence]

'What have I done now?'

[shrug]

'I can't apologise if I don't know what I've done.'

[silence]

'Please, Rosie, just tell me what I've done and I'll say sorry for it, whatever it is.'

R

Rosie started a spreadsheet of her own. Every quarter of an hour, she would update it with the total sum she had earned, sitting there and listening to Damien breathe through his mouth. As the total grew, she realised she would have enough to go away somewhere exotic. Rosie had thought she was going to be stuck in London all year, looking at photos of her school friends having fun online. Prague was the furthest she had ever been away from home. Now she had a better daydream for when Damien talked at her in his monotone about the wall clock being slow and how she should come back early from her lunch break, or Maya complained about the amount of translation work she needed to do instead of paying attention to Rosie.

R

Something hot and wet was dripping onto Rosie's neck. It ran down her clavicle and pooled in the little hollow that preceded her throat.

'What? What is it?'

'Nothing.'

'Just tell me why you're crying. I'm already awake.'

'You didn't even ask me. You just booked the whole trip and told me afterwards.'

'Was I supposed to ask you for permission? You said people should choose their own desires over their feelings at our age. That was why you refused to go out with me.'

'I could have given you my blessing.'

'What you mean is, you could have pretended to be OK with it, while still being really pissed off in private.'

'YES. THAT WAS EXACTLY WHAT I WANTED.'

'Your ex was right, you really should be on some sort of medication.'

M

It was not long past noon, but the scent from Sainsbury's fish counter already indicated that today's catch was past its best. Resting on a bed of ice behind the counter, Maya could make out elliptic furrows on individual shells, inlaid with blue and green. She hurried home, worried that the mussels would die, then twisted the corners of the ice trays frantically to get enough ice out of them into a bowl in which the mussels could rest while she prepared the sauce they would be cooked in. Then she washed them, yanking out the scraggly beards trailing from each shell. She threw away the ones that had opened when the others were closed, then the ones that closed when the others had opened. The smell of flesh and brine clung to her hands, even after she had scrubbed them twice. She did her make up and put on Carnival of the Animals quietly in the background. Then she sat at the table and waited for Rosie to arrive.

M

Rosie ate quickly, not looking up. When all the mussels were gone, Maya suggested that they exchange the gifts before pudding, to give themselves a chance to breathe. Rosie had bought a huge quantity of Maya's favourite chocolate bar. Maya suspected Rosie was trying to make sure she would comfort eat so much when Rosie left her that no one else would want her either. She did her best impression of pleased surprise and pushed the little blue box with the earrings across the table.

'Don't you want to try them on?'

'I thought you bought these for yourself.'

'No, they were always for you.'

'They're too nice, I can't wear them.'

'Of course you can, you'll look beautiful in them.'

'No, I'll just lose them. You should have got me something cheap.'

A pain shot from Maya's elbow, down towards the wrist. She didn't own an electric whisk and had whipped the egg whites for the macaroons by hand. She tried not to grimace. Rosie would say she was manipulative if Maya mentioned it, and then not understand that she'd made a joke.

'Shall we go out?'

'Where would we go?'

'We could go to the Muddler.'

'Why would I go there, I already have you?'

'We could go to the pub down the road.'

'I don't like the staff in there, they keep giving us evils.'

'You don't want to go out at all, do you?'

'No, I don't. I want to stay here and enjoy our anniversary.'

'Sorry I forgot, you're so fucking fragile going outside might break you. Why don't we just stay in here and read made up stories about the world instead?'

'I tried to tell you the truth when we first got together, and you didn't want to hear it.'

R

Rosie had to leave Maya another three times before it stuck. She went off to have as much fun as she could, on the other side of the world, where she didn't have to think about her ex-girlfriend or her manager or anyone else if she didn't choose to. Rosie knew she was looking for something, even if it wasn't clear what that was yet. She read the books that Maya had loaded onto her kindle, when she had still wanted to hear Rosie's thoughts on them. The people Rosie met in tiki bars and on bus tours of various natural wonders would listen politely to her talking about the books, but they usually changed the subject after a couple of minutes.

A few years later, Maya did write a story about her. Of all the people in the world, only she and Maya knew how much of it was truth and how much of it was lies.

Leon Craig is a writer from London who now lives in Berlin. Her work has been published in the *London Magazine*, the *White Review* and the *TLS* among others. Her debut short story collection *Parallel Hells* is forthcoming from Sceptre Books in 2021 and she is working on a novel.

Bed – Aoife Hanna

Silent you envelop me and take the day away. Weary body. Aching broken mind, repaired each night by you.

Countless lovers have lain here with us.

Each time we wonder if they'll be the last and when it almost feels like it – pray they're not.

Pulling back from precipice after precipice, the leap seldom worth the fall.

When I peel back your crisp white clothes and look upon your bareness there's a treasure map there with clues I can't quite solve.

A cipher all grey and dimpled, stains of menses, tattoos of spilled coffee; all that fuss forgotten. Who made that coffee? Was it me? Was it one of the transient guests? Or the one we loved?

Of all those that came and went, that we only knew once, or those with whom we shared a chapter; there's only one we wanted to be the last.

*

For months after her departure, mourning manifested itself in long strands of hair. 'Get used to it, my hair gets everywhere,' she'd said when our union was in its infancy. That sentiment caused mock annoyance.

Oh, how I long for them now.

Auburn, russet, peach, caramel, cinnamon, strawberry blonde.

Light bounced golden off them in my blotchy pink hand, but they were dark against your alabaster sheets,

A stark contrast of what existed and what we dreamt, fantasies of swollen bellies of families made.

Dreams that were projected onto her and those strands, shadow puppets with I the puppet master and you the stage.

As an unwilling audience watched in silence.

Yet now when I think of hot drinks and newspapers on chilly weekend mornings, valleys left in the dust on your iron bars from where silk scarves gripped.

Deep red welts on wrists no longer tied,
Of bodies being one.

We needn't have wished for more.

On the last day when she was adamant she wasn't to return to us, there was a frightening, blood-red sunset hanging low in the sky.

Unnatural, bloody, no part of that moment felt right.
But perhaps none of it ever did.

*

And so each day I come home to you, and there you are, inviting me to fall back down and back into the bleakness.

To bury my damp face into pillows which have long since lost her smell.

Aoife Hanna is an Irish writer and journalist based in the UK. Her words have featured in *Bustle*, *HuffPost*, *Metro*, *Delicious* and *Imperica*.

Three Weddings and a Marriage Equality Movement – Erica Gillingham

One way to tell my love story is this: I have been married three times in two countries to one woman.

This was not the original plan, but borders and voters and legal systems got in the way of any straightforward path to a federally recognised union. Others who fell in love when we did have similar stories. This is ours.

&

In the early years of university, it didn't seem possible that I was continually crossing paths with my future wife, Alex. She was the friend of my co-workers and my first girlfriend, the British girl at the parties whose references I understood just little bit better after the year I lived in Ireland. My first memory of Alex is at the Santa Cruz Boardwalk, where our university's college took over the beachside amusement park for the evening. I can picture her in the queue for the wooden roller coaster, laughing at some rude joke I'd just made. Fast-forward two years when I kiss her at a party unexpectedly and I see *fireworks*, but I don't have the where-withal to make a move. A year passes and I move into her house, needing a place to live for three months, and it's a matter of days before I decide there *is* something there. Just a few weeks later I confess that I'm in love with her – and I'm elated when she says she's in love with me, too. When she moves back to England two months later, I can only think of how I want to be with her – but marriage is not my first thought.

My home state, on the other hand, is preoccupied with marriage. California had begun pushing for legalising same-sex marriage with the 'Winter of Love' in 2004, when an estimated 4,000 couples were married in San Francisco after then-mayor Gavin Newsom ordered his offices to allow for same-sex marriage licenses. It was an exciting time in the city and, just an hour away at university, the bubbling atmosphere was felt in the class-room, too. Inevitably, those marriages were halted and invalidated, but then a series of court cases began. These eventually resulted in the California Supreme Court ruling that it was unconstitutional to ban marriage on the basis of sexual orientation, which legalised same-sex unions in the state of California in June 2008. But opponents were simultaneously organising in anticipation of the November Presidential election, working to put Proposition 8 on the ballot. Prop 8, as it became known, would alter the state constitution to define marriage as between 'one man and one woman', and it passed by a margin of four percent.

In the weeks prior to the election, bright yellow pro-Prop 8 signs with navy blue stick-figure heterosexual families were dotted around my conservative hometown. I passed them each day, even as we drove to cast our opposing votes at the county fairground polling station. Each sign I saw was in sharp contrast to the overwhelming sense of love – of *rightness* – that I felt in my relationship with Alex. With no organisation to join to fight against the proposition in my county, I rallied old friends to start a letter writing campaign to our local newspaper, telling our stories and sharing our reasons for voting against this amendment. Published in print and then posted online, we hoped we were changing people's minds. When the numbers came in on election night, it showed 60–70% of people in my county had voted in favour of Prop 8: I was crushed.

While all of this was happening, Alex and I were 5,128 miles apart. We'd had individual post-graduation plans, but those courses of action only lasted six months before we started looking into options for me to move to the UK. This made sense to us because, for starters, Alex had lived in *my* country, but I hadn't lived in *hers*; it only seemed fair that I would get to know about her home country, too. Second, even a cursory review of the UK immigration system showed, to my astonishment, that I could be considered a legal partner to Alex in multiple ways. These were options we could only dream about if she wanted to return to the US, but had lost her green card. Plus, in contrast to the vitriolic aftermath of Prop 8, the UK seemed like a more decent place to put down the foundations of our relationship.

&

This is where I admit that I moved with an engagement ring in my suitcase.

Hear me out. I was *so in love* and my home state was telling me *so loudly* that my relationship was invalid, rebelliousness couldn't help but kick in. That, and I couldn't imagine building a life without her. Also, my student visa was only good for fifteen months and, if we were going to get married, I knew Alex would need a year to plan the wedding. There are many ways to be romantic.

Having dreamt of this moment over months of long-distanced pining, I proposed to Alex in the spring on the Cornish cliffs under the tree where we had carved our initials. Her parents were in on the surprise, waiting around the corner with strawberries and champagne.

Wedding planning began almost immediately. Three options were on the table: the elegant Cornish wedding, the country California wedding, and the trendy London Town Hall wedding. Each had their own appeal, but only two of them would be legal. The UK had begun registering (same-sex) civil partnerships in December 2005,[†] and a civil partnership would grant me immigration rights as well as have the satisfaction of sending a demonstrative rebuttal to detractors back home. At the same time, California was where we fell in love, and where our large friend group and my even larger extended family lived.

In the end, we had two hometown weddings, and what weddings they were. For our first, we had glorious late spring weather as the backdrop to our Victorian hotel ceremony – and when we were announced as civil partners, we whooped in glee! Our legal document in hand, we were ready to celebrate with champagne, afternoon

---

† I can still remember the photographs of Shannon Sickles and Grainne Close of Belfast on the front pages of Irish newspapers when I lived in Galway. Such joy!

tea, and lashings of clotted cream. Later, with the Town Crier and a Cornish bag pipe player, our party processed through the village to the local sailing club, where we ate and drank and danced until we were dripping in sweat late into the night.

For our second, we planned our ceremony on the very same county fairgrounds where I had cast my vote against Prop 8 and we listed our names on the giant marquee, visible for the whole town to see. My childhood best friend, now an ordained pastor, wrote and performed our ceremony. She began with this:

> *Dear beloved community, we are gathered here for a one true purpose. [. . .]*
> *We are here to make a marriage. To make a marriage in a place where we are too often told that one cannot, should not, and will not be made. Friends, we have work before us today, for together we shall be undoing all of that.*

With this ceremony and reception, we felt *married*. We had committed to one another before our community, and they had affirmed our love.

&

In the subsequent years, we watched individual states change their laws to legalise same-sex marriage, and waited on key decisions from the Supreme Court of the United States. First, Prop 8 was overturned in *Hollingsworth v. Perry* in 2012, allowing same-sex marriages to re-commence in California. Second, the Defense of Marriage Act was struck down in *United States v. Windsor* in 2013, in which Edie

Windsor won her case for her New York state marriage to be recognised by the federal government.

And still, we waited. We didn't know how a California marriage license might affect our UK civil partnership, and we didn't want to risk it or my immigration rights. We also knew that, if we wanted to move back to the US, we couldn't apply for a new green card for Alex until our marriage was recognised federally, a reality that weighed heavily on us.

&

The year after the Marriage (Same Sex Couples) Act came into effect in 2014 in England and Wales, my parents were coming to visit. By now, we'd established our London community (including a few precious godchildren!) and we wanted a reason to throw a party, introduce everyone, and celebrate. Buoyed by joyous news of Ireland's same-sex marriage referendum and fuelled by the desire to have all our paperwork in order for whenever the US decided to catch up, we applied to 'convert' our civil partnership to a marriage. As we told our friends the news, we joked that this was 'third time lucky' and that we would be getting our London Town Hall wedding after all.

On 26th June 2015, we had our appointment to register our intent to marry. The civil servant was a welcoming, avuncular man whose husband was from Cornwall, too, and we were made to feel at-home in an otherwise bureaucratic set of offices and regulations, knowing that we would return to these halls in a few weeks' time and be officially married – in at least one country. Paperwork completed in the chilly, stone building, we stepped out into bright afternoon sunshine and our phones began buzzing wildly after the lack of reception. What we saw was that in Washington, D.C., the Supreme Court had just ruled in *Obergefell v. Hodges*, declaring that the entirety of the United States would now perform and recognise same-sex marriages. We wept on the town hall steps as we read Justice Kennedy's majority opinion, knowing that soon – much sooner than we had even thought possible – we would be married in *both* our countries.

Erica Gillingham is a queer poet and writer living in London, England, via Siskiyou County, California. She is a bookseller at Gay's The Word, Books Editor for *DIVA*, Poetry Editor for *The Signal House Edition*, and has a PhD in queer young adult literature. Erica's forthcoming pamphlet *The Human Body is a Hive* will be published by Verve Poetry Press in March 2022.

The Old Castle – Cathleen Davies

The Old Castle was falling apart these days. The bricks were loose and the roof tiles were a death-trap. They kept the harsh, fluorescent lighting in the loos, and you could see the years of grime sticking where the sealant should have been around the sinks, heavy make-up streaked the mirror until you almost couldn't see yourself. They had a smoking area outside now, with heaters that never bloody worked. You either froze or burned your crown, there was no in between. They'd tried to spruce it up, but frankly I preferred the place dilapidated. It held more of a charm that way when you were sipping your Bacardi and coke, or else one of the new cocktails they'd introduced with names like 'blowjob' and 'wet pussy'. 'Gaping arsehole' was a personal favourite. Not that I was drinking much these days. Tonight, I wasn't drinking at all, something I planned to announce quite proudly with the little cotton wool ball taped to my forearm beneath my usual, toned-down, button-up shirt. You'd have thought at my age and with the prospect of sobriety I might have preferred to stay home, but Friday nights are meant for dancing and anyway, I'd promised.

'There she is,' our Roxanne called over, her arms raised

theatrically. Roxanne was already at the bar, a cigarette stuck to the dry skin on her lip. Ten years since the smoking ban and Rox still had to be reminded to take the damn things outside. It could've been dementia, but she still claimed to be a sensible forty-five (ha ha!).

The Castle used to be more dismal, and therefore much more beautiful. We made our own smoke-machine back then with the constant lighting up of fags. Course, everyone smoked in those days, and even if you didn't, it was important that you couldn't see what we were up to whenever lips would touch, and a hand would find a head, the front of two trousers pressing together. Then if the lily law stepped in, you'd time to spring away before they caught you at it. *Is it a crime to dance now, officer?* Not that it would prevent them banging you up anyway.

'What's it going to be then?' Rox asked in her usual husky tone. 'They've a new one called 'The Sucker'. Apparently it knocks you out flat.'

'A water, if you please' I said, with a hint of arrogance.

'What was that, ducky? I think you must've misspoke.'

'Aha! But no, doctors' orders!'

'Pah!' Roxanne, forever the dramatist, mimed spitting on the floor. 'Doctors. What do they know? I was told at twenty five that my lifestyle would kill me, and now look,' she waved a heavily braceletted and liver-spotted arm over her body, clad as it was in sequins and chicken feathers. 'Fit as a fiddle.'

'Apart from the hip-replacement.'

'Shhhhh! don't speak too loudly, darling. These children will begin to think I'm geriatric.'

From her bra, she flourished a lighter, raised it to her cigarette.

'Oi, outside!' called out an insolent child behind the bar, a twink with flopping hair straightened flat against his forehead.

'I'm just testing it!' Roxanne answered firmly. 'Come on,' she picked up her cocktail and dragged me to the drizzly outside steps. I was grateful to step out, despite the cold. A gaggle of women (actual women, mind; not old queens like us) were dancing and singing on the newly furnished karaoke machine, butchering some of the classics. From the looks of their outfits and the willy-shaped straws, it was someone's bachelorette. I never understood why hen-dos gravitate towards The Castle so readily. Straight women always assumed that 'gay' was synonymous with 'fun', and while they weren't wrong in their assumptions, it didn't half ruin the atmosphere. But then, who was I to complain? These clubs weren't for me anymore.

'So, tell me, why the water?' Roxanne lit up a cigarette. I rolled up my sleeve.

'Because, my love, you are speaking to a blood-giver. A donator. A medical inspiration, if you will. My body might have saved a life today.'

'At your age! Goodness. Poor fellow, who wants your blood?'

'As of this week, the United Kingdom, who have lifted the ban against gay men donating, thus allowing people like me to participate in much-needed philanthropy.'

'Excellent news, my darling' Roxanne said sarcastically, sucking on her cigarette. 'Although why you'd let those strangers perforate you, I will never understand.'

'Oh please, don't pretend you're not a fan of perforation by strangers,' I scoffed. 'Well at least you were at some point in your adolescence before the sinking of the Titanic.'

'How droll,' Roxanne replied, exhaling her smoke beautifully so that it curled in tendrils like the stems of wilting flowers. She threw the tab end on the floor, ground it under her heels, which were noticeably shorter these days, although one daren't utter the words *varicose veins.* 'How's my face?' she asked, splaying her fingers wide to frame it to the best of her ability. I remembered when Roxanne was the most beautiful man I'd ever seen, with high cheekbones and wide eyes the colour of coffee beans, and still beneath the powder I could see that she was beautiful, more beautiful in fact, because despite it all she had refused to cower down and yet, miraculously, against all odds, survived.

'You look awful,' I said.

'Fantastic,' she moaned. 'To the powder room. Onwards!'

The bathroom had once only been for men. Now, it was officially 'unisex', but there was still the single urinal stuck stoically to the wall, the holes drilled between the cubicles, now mostly there for humour's sake, archaic decorations to indicate long-passed debauchery.

'I can't see a thing in this mirror,' Roxanne tutted, while dragging her tan-coloured lipstick in the space between her liner, which had seemed to permanently stain her skin over the years. I leant between the sinks and watched her.

'You really needn't bother. We won't see anyone interesting tonight.'

'Lord, when do we ever? But you never know. Anyway,' she rubbed her lips together, separated them with a satisfying *pap.* 'I choose to look ravishing for myself, don't you know.'

The high-pitched hawks and squeaks that hurricaned towards the toilet door could only be the hen-do on a battle mission.

116

'Oooooh, I'm gonna wet meself,' one dressed up as a ballerina (ambitious for her physique) cried out while barrelling into the cubical. The others waited outside, taking up as much space as possible and making it difficult to vacate.

'Mate, you look stunning,' said an angel, a trifle condescendingly to Roxanne.

'Thank you, my love. You're not so bad yourself.'

'Are they real?' asked another, pointing to her breasts.

'Of course!' Roxanne croaked. 'I paid for them myself.'

The angel leant forward to grope them from the bottom, cupping the padding as though comparing mangoes at a market. They all laughed raucously, and I wanted so badly to intervene and remind these women, with their bitten down cuticles and darkened roots, that our Rox was old enough to be their grandmother, and they wouldn't want someone fondling her in a dirty old toilet now, would they?

'She's handsy!' Roxanne said, causing another cascade of cackles. 'You should be buying me a drink first, I mean, really. I'll have this one then,' she plucked the plastic cup out of a devil's hand and wandered off swigging. Through the plastic I could see the mucky blue that meant it was all sugar and aniseed, a Blowjob if I wasn't mistaken. The women were in fits of hysterics. They'd be telling this story for years. It may make it into the Maid of Honour's speech. *I can't believe that drag queen stole your drink!*

'Vile,' I said, as soon as we were out of earshot.

'And think! Your blood can save one of them. Now that they've decided we're not all contagious to the touch. Now, let's shake them off that machine. Shall I go with Donna Summer or Diana Ross?'

'Don't tell me you disapprove,' I said, rolling my eyes.

'Of Diana Ross? Why should I?'

'Of giving blood.'

'Oh, I disapprove of anything that limits the consumption of alcohol, you know me.'

I rushed to keep up with her as she stopped to flick through the songbook.

'But ultimately, this is an iconic day! Think about our *rights*,' I said.

'What rights? The right to save their lives? Oh, I suppose it's all very noble. But wasn't it so much more *fun* when we were degenerates? We might have been hiding in the sewers but we ruled them. This . . .' she stabbed her finger on the page. 'Is the one. Oh DJ . . .'

Roxanne scuttled off to make her request to the poor teenager who worked behind the decks, handing me her Blowjob en route. No doubt he had plans to be one of those musicians who played techno or electro or whatever they were calling it, and now he had to play some awful song from the fifties. I almost felt sorry for the chap.

When Roxanne walked on stage I felt the lights went dimmer. It definitely seemed quieter, but then why wouldn't it be quiet? The place was near empty. The DJ began playing her song, but she waved him down.

'Not yet, darling, wait for my cue.' The music stopped. She smiled at the non-existent crowd. In that moment, I could see what she was picturing as she scanned her eyes around this vacant, plastic room, full of shining lights and sticky drinks and overbearing heterosexuals. She was back, perhaps, to the way it was, when no one would have seen her for the smoke screen, and anyway, it was never good to see you but always *bona to vada your dolly old eek,* when everyone was your mother and the whole world, or at least the part we were in, was veiled in silk and lace with curtains drawn, and our blood was always spilt, but still, it was our own.

'Ladies, gentlemen, darlings,' Roxanne began. 'It's time for my final swan song.' She gestured to the DJ. The trumpets began to play.

Cathleen Davies is a queer writer from East Yorkshire, England. Her work has appeared in a number of magazines and anthologies including Dostoyevsky Wannabes' collection *Love Bites,* Vagabond's *Anthology for the Mad Ones* and Weasel Press's *Before it was Cool.* She also co-runs *Aloka,* a magazine for non-native English speakers. Her hobbies include drinking and complaining more than her characters do.

Stewards – Andrew F. Giles

The questions that we ask of the mountain are smoke or mist – the long wind. Nothing is an incredible revelation. Our fucked-up eking is bound to the shifts and tendrils of high fog as it oscillates down and back up the clefts in the peaks where the horses cling to the edge. Who speaks the words of culture here? Who hears them? Who will come, asked Lorca, and from where?

Green flesh. Green hair. When I left the cities to live in a hamlet in the cold northern mountains of a southern country, three feelings were quiet inside me: *queer* – a magical word, an enchantment of smile-stretched vowels and hard-earned difference; *rural* – a word that from my mouth softens up the Rs into semi-Ws, smells like my family dinner table – liver casserole, sounds like my sisters laughing at the wrongness of the way my mouth made words with Rs; *climate emergency* – I was saying it right, but what effect would I have on it? None of these feelings together were common in the place where I was. Is it also right, that even in claiming our identities, wherever they are, however they look, we never lose the fear of not being – and the profound desire to not be – ourselves? I'm not sure. Now is a time of fake truths and conspiracy theories. Lying is business, and sneakiness is self-protection. The poetic opaqueness was a challenge to kick into action beyond the three feelings that lived in me. They were just the questions of the apocalypse hanging overhead.

There is no doubt that queer folk have been stewards of the land in all places and at all times: the cavepeople at the museum; the temporal, emotional multiplicity of the indigenous two spirit people; country women; The Edward Carpenter Community. Needing to see this as a network of likeminded folk, I live a lot in the queer history of outsiders – like lovers in a constellation, we quite often meet in books or somewhere else on the page. Up here, like lots of queer rural folk, I exist in a virtual network of other tribe members, poetic or imagined, sometimes online, sometimes physical. There is a great expanse of hope and loneliness, because being a steward of the land means being a steward of a publicly dying planet which needing money prevents us from saving. Even more challengingly, recently this dying planet's principal species just got sick and paranoid, and the clamour for a cure, or a lie about a cure, makes radical decisions about living conditions (which may involve taking a look at how the exchange of money specifically leads to violence and deprivation, but that exchange of other things and actions is a valuable process) seem less significant, or downright insulting. There's a chamois buck on the peak's edge, peering down – this land is my land – I might be dangerous. So is this the culmination of our sophisticated, twenty-first century human condition? A sickness that renders us unable to knit multiple, conflicting ideas at a time together under pressure? If they are sicknesses, they will probably happen again and again, so we could live kindly and creatively with this goblin presence.

With our polar opposites living inside us, never resolved, without *culmination and termination points*, we could look out across a plateau that curves up or down at the edges until the next plateau, where the horses cling to the edge. I'm stealing from two naughty schoolkids, Deleuze and Guattari, who riddled in rhizomes and plateaus in part, at least, to unbuild the direction of History, to come and go within it rather than see it as a series of endings and beginnings. A queer network of outsiders. Here in the mountains there really are a thousand plateaus, though, and I'm scared of not being me, and I don't want to be me: 'I'm no longer me and my house isn't even my house' – Lorca. Yesterday, I walked up through the mountain pass, up further past the three old cabañas with their encircling walls broken down, through the old yew and holly wood where the trees have twisted into half-human shapes, through the valley where the wild horses graze and big bones lie strewn about after the wolves have fed, up to the high green plateau with the old stone lambing cairns with curved walls like ancient beehives or burial chambers, and I felt the three feelings inside me. They crept to my fingertips and toes and tingled like running ants. It's fun playing with capitalism like it's a mental illness, I guess, and it's useful to slip in and out of History without its resolute endings and identities that always fail. The wind is whistling. On the thousand plateaus the land looks at me, blankly, and tells me to go home and turn over the soil, produce more edible stuff, walk those five kilometres to the shop even less. I don't really like my neighbours, don't always like myself. My anxiety and depression are both magnified here and the self is minimized sometimes, because you're working and thinking about if you've got enough logs and that there will be enough logs forever in a sustainable way on the land you are steward of. There are thousands of empty villages in Europe where historically folk have lived sustainably and practiced stewardship of the land, because otherwise it runs wild. Even countryside that looks agricultural can be wasting away, the old ways not cleared, the woods and forests left to dwindle or fall into disuse from humans or pigs, a traditionally familial and generational network disappeared or moved to cities. But if those families won't return to the land, there are ways and people who will, displaced networks of folk with radical plans for the planet, or just a sense of urgency. Yet it's slow, quiet and hard work. We have our polar opposites living inside us.

Nothing is certain. Suddenly everyone was using bleach again and racing through surgical masks because it was the rules and feeling worried and paranoid about somehow making someone else sick or getting sick. Can't you see the wound I've got from my chest to my throat, asks Lorca. What about me? The green woodpecker reappears in the corner of my vision every day, dipping down on a diagonal to the woods. Then people started isolating themselves from the machine and making new networks online and in their heads. Time and history is just another malleable network which you can slip in and out of, finding, reading, exchanging with your tribe to create a different constellation of authority. But you're a dirty human, of course, and people and ideas will fail and you'll wake up at 6am in the same clothes you've been wearing for days to collect eggs and walk the dogs – you carry a trowel everywhere you go now, ever since the neighbor said your dogs were shitting all over the village and what kind of ecologist were you? And your garden's a mess, you want to do it like this, and you don't want to grow that, and what do you mean permaculture, that's just weeds. Green flesh, green hair. There is the unfinished henge of wooden beams, carved with symbols, that we built together, and whose meaning will be quickly forgotten. Your gods are dying.

Andrew F. Giles is a British-European writer of poems, reviews and creative non-fiction. He lives and works at Greyhame Farm in the mountains of northern Spain, a permaculture project, creative residency and safe space for queer folk and their allies.

Autumn is the Queerest Season – Serge Ψ Neptune

because the air is wet & slippery the men
so sickly beautiful & quick to burn
something boiling underneath the carpet
of porous orange on asylum road beside
the hydrangea smirking baba yaga's
chicken-legged houses suspiria-red windows
mature men in olive emerald obsidian jumpers
office suits walking to post-work grindr dates
by the vigorous maples reaching for the pallid sun
the men so sickly beautiful like deers shot
& slow-mo dropping sleeks of bronze fur carcasses
by brimmington park the young hipsters braving
the brisk air sleeveless hairy biceps walking
to post-gym grindr dates at queen's rd peckham
by the blackbird bakery birman cats stand in rows
as if to judge each tryst

& then it happens

the sweetest of voices sings men to the mire of
    their own mind
men walk towards the dark / pale fingers
pull them in / laughter is heard / still echoes

———————————

Serge ♆ Neptune has been called 'the little merman of British poetry'. His work has appeared in *Magma, fourteen poems, Impossible Archetype, Queerlings, Finished Creatures, perverse,* whynow, *harana poetry, Lighthouse, Banshee, Spontaneous Poetics, Brittle Star,* Ink Sweat & Tears and Strange Poetry. His first pamphlet, *These Queer Merboys* is published with Broken Sleep.

Danny, The Wild Kids and
Abba – Wayne Blackwood

Only Abba and Danny would know the truth of what happened on the night of the fourteenth of December. When Johnson got word of the incident the very night it happened, he gave Danny a beating that he was sure to remember and kept him inside for weeks.

Danny had barely turned seven years old when he was prematurely yanked from Granny's sheltering bosom and hauled under Johnson's boots to live with him. Danny never called him Daddy, he never naturally developed the habit. They lived in a very tiny house – in the most ratchet *tenement yard*‡ at 48 Marl Road in Rockfort, East Kingston – furnished with one miniscule bed, which filled the entire room. There was also a very tiny stove, a what-not, two small dressers, a wardrobe, a large barrel for miscellaneous storage and a small basket for dirty laundry. Johnson, standing at six feet tall, lived there with his

‡ A multi-family housing arrangement consisting of many substandard dwellings packed closely on a single plot of land. Dwellings often share resources such as running water and toilets.

overweight high school sweetheart and now common law stay-at-home-wife, Erica. She was Danny's new stepmom, though she was no good at it.

Nine other families of tenants lived over at 48 Marl Road and they all had on average five kids. All the tenants shared outside showers and toilets – which were lined off in a row like those at a public gym. None of the tenants ever volunteered to clean the toilets. They would only wipe, then pad the seats with layers of toilet paper before doing their business. To flush the toilet, they needed a bucket that they would fill with water at the standpipe in the middle of the yard.

Depending on when they went, there might have been a queue, because the stand pipe served as the only water source for all nine families and by the time they returned to flush there'd perhaps be two more persons added to the previous three that were patiently waiting to use the toilet.

The tight walls of the showers were covered in green slime that built up over time and ran down like oil. You had to constantly twist and turn and bend and stoop to properly clean yourself and to avoid rubbing your shoulders or any other unfortunate body part against the sticky walls. Some of the women who lived in the tenement yard were heavily plump (Erica especially) and Danny always wondered how they managed to take comfortable and unhindered showers.

The home change was so sudden – right at the beginning of the school year – that it left Danny disoriented and confused. He developed a stammer until he was about twelve years old and could never look anybody in the eyes. He however remained exceptionally intelligent and sharp for his age.

Danny had *pepper grain*[§] hair and was very lanky compared to the other seven-year-olds. His body dragged itself behind a big head bent low. He resembled a dead puppet. To make matters worse, he had big, white, overgrown teeth – way too big for his mouth and so everybody took to calling him Bugs Bunny. Bugs Bunny was his only cute nick-name; the community would soon brand him with a plethora of hateful ones.

In that tenement yard, the rabies infested, unsterilized mongrel dogs marked their territory on every doorstep. The smell of piss, shit – of both man and beast –, sewage water, curry chicken back, tin mackerel, weed and cheap perfumed lotions were all natural aromas in that ecosystem. The *cayliss gal dem*[¶] who lived there would get up every day and cuss each other until night, forgetting to feed their hungry children. None of the men worked formal jobs, except for Johnson, but he worked very odd and late hours and was rarely at home.

Danny went into survival mode when he noticed just how unnatural his new habitat was for him, compared to the life of comfort he had known at Granny's; so, like every other living organism, he had to now adapt and evolve to survive. He remembered reading a short passage somewhere in an encyclopaedia that whales were once land mammals. He recalled it word for word: *'Vertebrates evolved in the sea and eventually moved onto land. The ancestors of whales later returned to the sea, taking advantage of its rich food supplies. As early whales adapted to their new marine surroundings, a diversity of species evolved.'* That is how he too must now evolve, blend in and

---

§ Tiny balls of hair that appear in short afro-hair when it is not combed/brushed often.

¶ Women who display lude or lascivious behaviour.

make friends with the wild kids running bare-chested and barefoot on the concrete in this tenement yard.

At first, Danny made friends quite easily and had never before experienced so much freedom to run wild with no supervision. Granny was a much more vigilant guardian than his step-mother Erica, so he seized this opportunity and became a bare-chested wild kid himself. He spent a lot of time with the other kids climbing trees (though he was really bad at it), playing *HopScotch, Dandy Shandy, Police and Thief, Chiney Skip, Mama Lashy, Hide and Seek, Bend Dung and Stucky***, baseball and so many other outdoor games that required a lot of energy and no expensive equipment.

They were very crafty, these wild kids, who made and flew big kites, constructed trucks out of juice boxes, match sticks, bottle corks and thread. They made *bingys*†† and hunted birds, mostly pigeons. When they had piped water in abundance, they would play water-wars then hide from their parents to avoid the beating they were sure to receive as soon as they returned home. They often teased passers-by, mostly old men and famed *Obeah*‡‡ women. They even stoned mango trees on Norman Terrace on their way home from school (they all went to the same primary school). When the pack of wild kids started coming up the terrace, the squeals of dogs they also stoned announced their approach and they would always get into a fight or two with other kids from other schools.

Years passed and when Danny was ten, he had learned

** Children's games played in Jamaica.

†† Slingshot. A projectile launching weapon made from a Y-shaped branch or piece of wood or elastic material. They are commonly used to hunt birds and other small game.

‡‡ Jamaica version of 'Voodoo'.

all the slangs and codes of his peers. All the kids in the yard played together, except when their respective parents were at odds and not speaking. Johnson and Erica usually kept their heads down, but that didn't stop the other boys from hesitating to play with Danny. The overly graceful limp in his wrist and the sophisticated, refined way that he walked stunted his adaptability to this new environment.

These things he failed to notice about himself because he wasn't doing them on purpose, but others – children and adults alike – perceived them in him and scrutinized him. For those reasons, the other boys deemed him unsuitable to evolve and truly become a wild kid. Danny soon became an outcast who was no good for cricket, football or any other sport dominated by the boys. He excelled however, at all the games that the girls loved. The boys stopped picking him for their teams and no longer wanted to play with him. Except Abba.

Abba was suspiciously light-skinned, because his parents and sister were of a much darker hue. He had shoulder-length sunburnt dreadlocks because his father was a rastaman. Whenever Abba was in the sunlight his head would glow and give him a halo – like a Rasta Jesus. He was twelve years old and in Danny's eyes he was perfect.

Being the king of the ghetto playground jungle, Abba was the most agile, the most athletic and the most respected. When none of the other wild kids would pick Danny for cricket or football because he couldn't hold the bat or kick the ball, Abba would. When the other boys wanted to beat up Danny, Abba stood between them.

Danny tried so hard to fit in, but his efforts were futile: you have to be born a wild kid to be one and he was an expatriate. Nonetheless, he was determined to change, and this change was going to come through Abba. Abba would shield him and integrate him and the other wild kids could do nothing to stop that. For a moment, it worked, the wild kids saw him as one of their own, until the fourteenth of December.

It was just another evening after the wild kids had done playing. Abba, his sister and Danny were playing cards on their shared veranda waiting for their dads to come home. Danny wasn't ready to go to his house, which was the door next-door, because Erica was never going to let him watch his cartoons; at this hour she usually watched The Murray Show. Furthermore, he was free, he had already eaten, and Johnson wasn't there.

After thirty minutes of joking around on the veranda, Abba's sister left to go eat at their auntie's house, which was the door right after Danny's. Not long after she left, the boys heard five gunshots right outside the gate. Danny quickly followed Abba into his house. They weren't scared because they'd heard gunshots before, and they were almost sure that the gunmen wouldn't come into the yard. Abba reassured Danny that it wasn't a shootout and that the men were probably simply testing the guns.

Abba jumped onto his bed and casually signalled Danny to lay next to him. Abba tossed the deck of playing cards above their heads, and the boys laughed hysterically as the cards came swirling down. Danny gathered a few of them and up they went again. Then down they came again. Then up. Then down. Then out of the blue, they kissed. Danny's heart pulsated to the rhythm of a million horses galloping across a plain (he liked western movies). A mix of emotions rushed through his body as if he were lying under the heavy flows of Dunn's River Falls in St. Ann Parish (he'd been there only once). His body palpitated rapidly at Abba's touch. His touch. Bad touch. Good touch. Danny was confused, but didn't want the touching to stop. Only Abba existed and the sound of guns being tested faded into the background and became like the sound of downtown Kingston's January 1st fireworks.

Danny had no real idea what homosexuality was. All he knew was that he always wanted to be close to Abba, but this was truly the furthest thing from his mind. He'd been introduced to a world he never imagined could've existed. After the kiss, Abba pulled down his shorts and told Danny to touch *it*. Danny refused. Danny felt like Abba was inviting him to touch the green slime on the bathroom walls of their tenement yard. Something churned in his stomach and his brows furrowed that Abba would suggest such a thing. Hell was a place he often heard Granny talk about, but he never stopped to ponder it. Now, all of a sudden, he felt like Abba was inviting him to hell.

Abba was upset and made his disappointment known that Danny didn't do as he had asked. Dismayed, he was putting it away. The fear of never again being his friend gripped Danny. He did not want to lose his protection, his attention or his affection. So, his hand swiftly moved to oblige, but in a split second it fell to his side again, because something did not feel right about it. He eventually forced himself to touch it for longer, but he could not bring himself to the ten seconds mark.

Seeing this, Abba exploited Danny's weakness and vulnerability and became even more exigent. When it became unbearably painful for young Danny, tears filled his eyes and he decisively refused. Abba was shaken, his lost mind returned to his body, he looked afraid. He got up, went outside and told his older cousin his version of what had happened. To this day, Danny has never understood the logic of it all. They were friends no more after this. Abba avoided him by all means possible.

When Johnson got word of the incident the night it happened, Danny witnessed shame, anger and hate in his eyes. Johnson beat him so that everyone in the yard could hear that he was being punished for his disgusting acts. Danny would never forget the date, because while Johnson beat him with the usual old leather belt with the rusted buckle, he never stopped repeating, '*today is de fourteen ah Dicembah, ah today mi ago kill yuh an hide yuh body, cause I not raising no battyman!*'

Danny received a lash with each syllable for thirty minutes. He might have died if Granny didn't come in time to save him. Johnson barely looked at or spoke to Danny for weeks after that. Abba's father didn't beat him and no one teased Abba.

Abba, his cousins and the wild kids spread the news throughout Rockfort, East Kingston and quickly made up their own exaggerated versions of what took place on the fourteenth of December. One account claimed that Abba was sleeping and that Danny snuck into his room to spy on him. Years later, other versions surfaced. Danny 'learned' that they were playing karate, Abba's member fell out and Danny lunged towards it.

Only Abba and Danny knew the truth about what happened that night. Abba was barely able to look at Danny while the other boys teased and threatened him mercilessly (Abba often joined in). From that night and for years after that, Danny was called a '*chi chi man*', '*fish*', '*battyboy*' and 'faggot' and no one remembered the name Bugs Bunny.

Since then, none of the wild kids dared to queue for the showers and toilets when Danny was there. It was as if he was branded with a Scarlett B, for *'Battyman'*. Danny's head hung lower and deeper into his books, his body grew lankier, and his stammer developed a stutter. His teenage years were even more unbearable and he suffered assaults, abuse and unwelcomed advances from thugs (who denied being gay).

Today is again the fourteenth of December; Danny has just turned twenty, eleven days ago. Danny is on his way to Granny's when he sees the hearse and the crowds outside the SDA church at the intersection of Marl Road and Norman Terrace. He inquires and someone shows him the programme. In disbelief, he hastens to verify that it is not a hoax. His shaking legs carry him to the wooden windows of the church, they refuse to bring him any further. From where he stands, he has a good glimpse of the corpse at the pulpit with sunburnt dreadlocks that once carried a halo.

Life is so fucking unpredictable. He trembles as he struggles within himself to not run into the church and shake the corpse awake. He so badly wants to go inside and at least pay his respects, but he knows it wouldn't be wise. All the former wild kids are there and every chance they get, no matter where they see him, they never waste the opportunity to mock and threaten him; no one could forget battyman Danny's story. They just don't remember today's date, so they can't see the irony.

They don't know that this was the night Abba betrayed Danny. The night their friendship ended. The night of Danny's first kiss and the horrors associated with it. The night he almost died at the hands of his father, had Granny not hidden him under her long skirt. The night he found out that his father would never truly love him again. The night that he discovered that he was a *battyman and battyman fi dead.*

Still, this date could never miss Danny, for it was the day he had been broken by the one person in the world he thought understood him most, and this happened just eleven days after his birthday and eleven days before Christmas. Every Christmas for him since then had been prefaced with a certain anger and sorrow.

He peeps through the church's wooden windows as he reminisces on his distant, fading memories with Abba and the good fun they had at 48 Marl Road. Abba never left the tenement yard. Danny wonders how things might have turned out if he had done everything exactly like Abba asked. Maybe Abba would not have told his cousin, or maybe they would have been friends and secret lovers to this day. Maybe he would have also followed Abba into the gang, got shot like he did or maybe Abba would have taken a different path and would still be alive.

That night, Abba might have felt too guilty, too ashamed and too afraid. He must have thought that Danny would have said something to someone, so he had to act first. Nevertheless, today Danny stands at the wooden windows, deliberating within himself, blaming himself and finding every way possible to try and exonerate Abba. Suddenly, while standing at the window – the wild kids eternally separating him and the faded halo – he discerns that he had loved Abba, the entire time, ever since he was ten and he still does.

It was just three weeks ago that he last saw Abba alive. It was on Windward Street at about midday. They were heading in opposite directions on the same pavement.

They both stared intently into each other's eyes up until they passed one another. Abba must be twenty-two years old now, Danny thought to himself. His hair still glowed in the sun and he still looked like a Rasta Jesus, except he had no beard.

Danny noticed that Abba faintly smiled at him: it was time for closure. They were finally about to exchange words after ten years. Abba was going to apologise and treat Danny kindly (they're mature adults now). However, Danny stopped, looked back and waited, but Abba did not.

Wayne Blackwood is a Jamaican who moved to Toulouse, France in 2016. His short stories are intimate, engaging, and thought-provoking with a vibrant and poetic realism. He is currently working on his first collection of short stories focused on his lived gay experiences in the island of Jamaica.

This Whole Heart
Treasure – Debra Lavery

In the morning, she bids me first to lace her hair
    with scarlet ribbons,
To brush it so that sunlight flashes in the richness
    of its ripples.
She bids me lace her 'til her waist is cinched and neat,
She bids me pat her, dab her, smooth her 'til she's sleek.

My lady bids me buff her pale, cold bosom
With the powder that will make it glisten.
Then she bids me lay her golden locket softly
In the valley of her breasts.

I lace her corsets good and tight as she directs me,
I see her wince a little as I pull.
But we are both together in this moment as it should be,
Her eye approves me as I tighten her in place.

At last, my mistress bids me gravely button up her boots,
Beneath my hands the tight black leather creaks.

I hear her sigh with gentle pleasure in my work,
She rests her hand upon my head and goes her way.

In the evening, she is weary from her work,
As the shadows underneath her eyes may give away.
But I do stroke the bruises from her icy skin most gently.
I know some hands are not as tender quite with her
    as mine.

As I ready her for bed her skin begins to shift and stipple
Beneath the brushing of my fingertips.
But yet her face remains both hard and fragile.
Her life has made her so she never will admit defeat.

Sometimes I see my lady watching my reflection in
    her glass,
Whiles I do brush her hair an hundred times before
    she goes to bed.
The licking candle flame reveals the liquid kindling
    in her eye then,
And I am sure that this is when she loves me best.

Then I do lay her lovely limbs within the bed,
And stroke her hair until her eyes begin to close.
And so at last another weary day for her is over,
She knows that I will watch her as she sleeps.

If anyone had told me I should find this heart
    full pleasure
To serve a lady cold and dignified as she,
I would not believe that I would be permitted
To find such happiness before her on my knees.

Debra Lavery was born in West Sussex and is now based in Hertfordshire. After a degree in French and English and a variety of occupations, she is now an English teacher in North London by day and writes poetry and fiction whenever she gets time off from marking essays.

The Human Lottery
Ticket – Fox Francis

At some point in the meeting, Juliet realises she has entirely stopped listening. Instead, her focus has been drawn to the boots of the man sitting opposite her, currently resting on the edge of the table, muck clinging to the soles. He must have been in the countryside, or perhaps walking his dog, she thinks. There is no nature here.

The very fact that he can lounge in this room, feet inches from the sliced fruit, would have once amazed her. Now, it doesn't touch her, which isn't to say it means nothing. More, she understands this man is her peer, her equal, and yet he feels the need to stretch out his body, make himself feel big. She should pity him. She looks at the walnut table, the matching chairs, remembers the design being commissioned for the company by the founder. She wonders if the furniture feels solid under his sprawled limbs, if it is in fact the only thing propping him up.

The night before she and Nic had argued. A manifestation of Sunday night fears, seemingly the only space in the week for their emotions to escape, rising up like thin wisps of smoke that warn of the blasting furnace beneath. In the transitioning hours between their personal and professional lives, one of them had let it slip that they were unhappy. She isn't even sure if it was her or Nic who spoke, but wants to acknowledge in a way it doesn't matter because of course they are both unhappy, how could anyone of sound mind be happy entrenched in the lives they led? They worked, they slept. Sometimes they remembered to feed each other. Sometimes they decided to starve each other. They couldn't possibly be alone.

The man doesn't look at anyone in the room, nothing has been said to warrant his eye contact.

Instead, he cranes his neck to study the murky-blue glass of a neighbouring tower. She imagines him captivated, narcissus and his pool. Yet she has done the same in these meetings, stared out of the window so long that she wished she were one of the birds cruising by.

She used to wish to be the window cleaner, her world and his divided by inches of reinforced glass and just about everything else. Even that feels too constricting now, to be of human form with duties and obligations and institutions. Better to be a bird. A bird-brain. Better to be a piece of furniture. A chair has a singular purpose. A chair could reach nirvana simply by being sat on. Was her marriage ending? The thought sits for a moment, entirely still and then dissipates.

The man is scrolling through images on his phone. Dog. Dog. Naked woman. Dog. Beheading GIF. His thumb ticks in a familiar movement. Mindless and dismissive, she recognises it from dating apps. Perhaps this posturing is just another thing to do, a parlour game to hold his intel-lect in place while they blink toward the artificial lights and Monday morning EBITDA. This is perhaps his most compelling contradiction; an insecurity with no foundation that she can detect. If he had been hopeless, idiotic and without merit, he could posture all he wanted and she would laugh, perhaps not take note at all. Why, in such a position of privilege and power did he still need validation from the people who worked beside him? He hadn't even learned their names.

And does Nic suddenly expect to be happy, she wonders. What did that even mean? Happiness was optimistic, naïve. Happiness was a goal for your twenties and a pipe-dream for your thirties. Wasn't now the time to let it go? Surely they were too old for happy. Too wise. Better to be content, to be known, to look at the face of another person and find comfort and familiarity in the lines and creases. A warm body to curl up against at night. At least that is what she would argue for, the known world.

Why then, had she leapt from their bed last night, as if she had been struck, and deposited herself in the guest bedroom? Something Nic said, or perhaps a look, a particularly enraging look.

She had pulled pillows from the storage cupboard and wrestled with sheets to dress the guest bed while Nic stood wordlessly in the doorway, her arms folded over her chest, obscuring the lettering on an old T-shirt, a souvenir from a marathon Juliet had ran in a previous decade. At that moment Nic looked like a child just woken, her face too weary to hold any expression, instead just waiting for the scene to end, for permission to return to bed.

All sense of reason lost, she had pushed past Nic, down the stairs and out of the front door. Within moments she found herself standing in the garden, fists balled tightly, the skin on her chest prickling with indignation. The house loomed. Underfoot, the soil felt damp, or perhaps just very cold. She waited, only half aware she was holding her breath until Nic flicked off the porch light. A final fuck-you and the first punctuation in a shared stream of consciousness that has lasted all evening, or perhaps the entirety of their relationship.

Nic sleeps on her stomach. Nic thinks the worst thing in the world is a dusty sex toy. While other people eat with their eyes, Nic explores the world through her mouth. Nic would rather go hungry than eat the same thing two days in a row. On the motorway at night, Nic sometimes closes her eyes on the long straights. Nic is Patti Smith. Nic is Zac Efron. Nic has played Jazz Guitar since she was twelve, but now only picks up an instrument when the house is empty. Nic takes strangers to the most romantic restaurant in the world, just for a reason to dine there. Nic curses when she's happy. Nic becomes overly formal in an argument. Nic can get lost in a supermarket but makes her way through the winding streets of Rome at night, without a map. Nic thinks ladybirds are unlucky. More than anything, Nic wants to be able to make you laugh. As a child, Nic spent hours alone, carefully cataloguing her possessions as a way to pass the time. Nic hasn't smoked in thirty-nine months. Nic still says mix-tape when she means playlist. Nic worships the sun as if the radiating heat of sunburn were something akin to love. Nic is an expert at living in invisible prisons. Nic reads Google News from bottom to top, starting with Entertainment and working her way up to World Affairs. She says it is the only way she can ease into the world. Nic doesn't believe in decaf. Nic insists on sleeping with the window open, even in winter, even in a basement in Harlem. Nic dreams in International Klein Blue. Nic sometimes buys books just to confirm her suspicion that they are terrible. Nic buys fresh cut flowers in case a visitor drops by. Nic buys tins of sardines decorated with traditional illustrations for all her friends, even the vegans. Nic has fallen in love twice in her life, the first time with her mother. Nic hates the internet and insists that anything experienced through a screen starves the other senses. Nic still watches pornography, but only in a hurry. Nic still eats junk food, but only in a hurry. Nic keeps old fashion magazines and when she pushes through the stacks searching for something they make the same silken sound as mixing mah-jongg tiles. Nic is Robert Mapplethorpe. Nic is Billy Crystal. Nic has a brother who has been dead longer than he has been alive. Nic's first band appeared in *Melody Maker*, but an unhappy ex destroyed her only copy of the magazine. Nic uses two alarm clocks, even on holiday. Nic was made to memorise classical poems at boarding school and can still place each piece of punctuation, each word. Cary Grant makes her flinch. Jimmy Stewart makes her laugh. Nic can walk for hours without complaint, perhaps days. Nic taught herself about physical pleasure one summer holiday, Sonic Youth on the cassette player, and somewhere under that, the sound of the neighbour mowing their lawn and the smell of cut grass tumbling through her bedroom window. Nic is a devious card player. Nic has sat on a beach in Bali, eating hand-caught fish, the memory of biting straight into the raw flesh so far from her life in suburbia, it feels like a dream. Nic has spent weeks in rehab. Nic has spent months in bed. Nic is happiest at an outdoor concert; the genre of music is of no consequence. Nic can never name the bands she was in. Nic is a human lottery ticket. Nic is usually late, but somehow makes her presence feel all the more like a gift. Nic believes in spirits, but only Irish ones. Nic played with dolls until she was twelve. When she was thirteen she realised she was gay. Nic is not Hillary Rodham Clinton. Nic is not Nick Cave, but perhaps she is a Bad Seed.

Juliet will go home this afternoon and make love to her wife. She will unbutton Nic's starched shirt and tenderly kiss at her neck and breasts until she and Nic are both teary and sweaty, mouths full of apologies. Nic will forget all about happiness or unhappiness and they can slip back under the surface of their lives. She will leave the office a little early, she will change the sheets in preparation for Nic's return. The cotton will feel cool to the touch and smell of fabric softener. Perhaps she will detour on her way home and pick up a fresh meringue from the little place in Bermondsey. A fresh meringue piled high with redcurrants. These are things Nic will appreciate.

She looks over to the man. He is watching a tiny football match play out on his phone. The figures barely more than strips of moving colour, an expressionist painting come to life. One side a lurid yellow, barely contained by the screen, the other a deep maroon like oxidised blood.

The meeting has ended and only they remain in the boardroom. Two partners in the same firm. He isn't able to acknowledge her in any way. The pair of them sit, together yet apart, and she finds herself matching her breathing to his. Sensing no movement, the overhead lights switch to energy saving mode.

Juliet is happiest outdoors. Juliet looks great in cashmere. Juliet wakes at five each morning and watches the sunlight edge across the bedroom. Juliet is a lousy traveller. Juliet weeps when she hears her childhood teacher has hanged himself, asking why she hadn't been there for him, even though they last spoke when she was eleven years old. Juliet is a grown woman. Juliet still looks for wisdom in the lyrics of Neil Young, the art of Jasper Johns. Juliet pays the bills on time. Juliet buys men flowers. Juliet made partner at just twenty-eight years old. Juliet googles *new things to do with asparagus.* Juliet googles *silent ischemia.* Juliet googles *marathon masturbation club (lesbian edition).* Juliet never remembers her dreams. Juliet winces when men ask her, *you and me, babe – how about it?* Juliet is always right. Juliet knows what to do. Juliet is Billie Eilish. Juliet is the notorious RBG. Juliet runs marathons she hasn't trained for. Juliet arranges furniture and flowers, fundraisers and funerals. Juliet doesn't believe in jet lag. Juliet is just like everyone else. Juliet is an only child. When Juliet opens Finder on her Mac, she is confronted with a picture of an ex that she stole from Facebook years ago. Juliet dresses in lawsuits. Juliet buys art made by strangers and ethical meat that can be sourced back to the farm. Juliet sends her warm regards. Juliet finds her thighs patterned with mystery bruises. Juliet sings off-key. Juliet calls her parents on Sunday afternoons, puts the phone on speaker and starts the washing up. Juliet follows the ballet with unwavering attention. Juliet eats other executives for breakfast. Juliet lives for brunch. Juliet has no interest in penetration. She is Thom Yorke's wife. She is Brian Keenan's son. Juliet has medical scans of her right wrist, her teeth and her womb. She doesn't know how to ethically dispose of them, so they sit in a drawer in the guest bedroom and she must remember to move them anytime visitors come to stay. Juliet tells colleagues she's an empiricist. Juliet pays buskers to stop playing. Juliet looks at instagram in the bath. Juliet finds it hard to climax on a work day. Juliet has two parents who love her very much. On her bedside, Juliet keeps a book entitled IF YOU'VE SEEN IT ALL, CLOSE YOUR EYES. Juliet excuses her entire youth with the sweeping statement, I was young; I needed the experience. Juliet stays up on election night. Juliet tells interns no matter how stupid you feel, remember Little Red Riding Hood couldn't tell a talking wolf from her own grandmother. Juliet won't let you go to voicemail. Juliet used to make people cry in boardrooms and bathrooms, but she's learned better now. Juliet grew up in a bungalow with no central heating and a faulty septic tank. Juliet's favourite word is tender. Juliet's favourite taste is blood from a steak. Juliet is Boudica, enraged and enthralled. Juliet is the sun. Juliet is someone's wife. Juliet willingly submits but will never succumb. Juliet remembers how to have fun.

Juliet has come home early, but not thought to check with Nic's plans. Now she is alone, for the first time in how long? It's a strange sensation, the silence almost a low hum, somehow a surprise that the house exists beyond the two of them being in it. She isn't used to waiting for other people.

The house is still in the afternoon, a sentinel powered down. Without Nic the house carries almost no discernible meaning. The books, the art, the ephemera. All articulations of the relationship. A shrine to a life shared. The meaning of home is Nic herself. She'd go mad if she had to stay here alone, better to burn it all down. Better to live in a sailboat. Or curl her body up like a fern, form a forest in the library.

The meringue sits on the kitchen table. Stiff and white, an expectant bride. The sheen on the redcurrants makes them appear artificial. She picks one up, rolls it between her thumb and forefinger, easing the fruit, increasing pressure until the skin splits and the pulpy flesh bulges open. She doesn't need to put it in her mouth to summon the acrid sensation on her tongue. Juliet pictures Nic leaning against the unit in the kitchen, half wrapped in a sheet, the slash of her pelvis digging into the granite worktop, her shoulder blades sharp and exposed. A hand at her mouth with a second bite of meringue already pressed to her lips as she chews at the first. She would swear Nic has never eaten a meal without devouring it. Nic eats as if she has never tasted before, as if she is only now just discovering pleasure. Flashes of teeth as she savages an orange, biting and sucking at the flesh. Juliet tries, really tries to recall the aspects of Nic's body. Her wiry black hair, now curdled grey, her sharp, angular jaw tilted out accusingly or cracked open wide in moments of ecstasy.

Even now, there is something about their bodies touching that reunites them in a way words cannot. Not libidinal, something deeper. There in childhood but also predating it, almost instinctual, as if the same sensation is held by tiny mammals curled up together in burrows and warrens. The absolute peace of touch and being touched by someone you love. The warmth of bare skin. *Everything is all right* it says, *I am here with you*. Let the world rage on outside.

She wants to show Nic her appreciation. To be tender and thoughtful. To feel awake and alive when she is at home with her wife, not half-lost to the world of work, assaulted by emails, headlines and deadlines.

Juliet also thinks of the art intern. How she finds opportunities to stop at her desk and give encouragement. Most recently, she found herself leaning over the intern, close enough to smell her conditioner, and increasing the point-size of the text in the intern's art file. Take up space, she says, holding eye contact for as long as she deems appropriate in a work environment. Is the intern queer, she wonders. Even if she were, the intern is young enough not to have to identify through labels, to restrict her sexuality through words. If she does, the intern has the choice of over fifty titles to ascribe to her gender identity and sexuality on her chosen social network. What would it be to live freely now? To have youth and bravado and more freedom of expression? Could she have that still? Take it for herself, but how to start?

Juliet pushes a finger through the crust of the knotted pavlova, deeper and deeper, ignoring the gooey resistance until she reaches her knuckle, then she pulls back, leaving a wound in its side. She sits a few moments longer until both her phones start vibrating at once, her personal hand-set jerking violently as if in death throes, the professional one seemingly tap dancing away to avoid a similar fate of execution. She turns the phones over like tarot cards, one at a time, revealing the screens. A reminder to visit the hygienist. A strategic review at seven p.m.

Even with Juliet in it, the house remains empty. Nic does not come home.

Fox Francis is a non-binary writer living in South East London. They write to feel closer to other people.

The Wall – Len Lukowski

Our friendship died in a fancy eatery in Hebden Bridge, amongst yummy mummies and Londoners visiting their second homes. Funny we got buried there, given the places we used to go.

The eatery was packed. A harassed-looking sixteen year old was the only visible member of staff. You clicked your fingers to get her attention and snapped when she did not know all the dishes by heart. You scolded her with such venom for delivering your Rustic Terrine Forestière too slowly that I could see her eyes well up. I looked at you, trying to decipher whether anything remained of the person I'd spent years of my life obsessed with, and had to admit no such person existed, maybe never had. As I began gathering my stuff you asked where I was going, confused at first, then desperate. Your face turned purple with anger and your own eyes started to mist. I felt torn about leaving, cruel even. I was the last person left who still cared about you and what I'd seen earlier that day made me realise you needed help. Then I looked again at the waitress and decided I couldn't be the one to help you.

*

Do you remember the first time I went round to your house, Natalie? Oh man, I do. It was an unusually sunny winter's day in Leeds ten years ago. My fingers and toes were cold as zombies but the sunlight cut through everything. I was nineteen and in love in a way I don't think it's possible to be when you're older. Kissing on your bed as we listened to The Pixies felt like a happiness I'd never dared to hope for. I wasn't so long out of school, and you know what they did to me there. To discover someone could actually love me blew my mind.

The night we met I was in love with Maria. I guess I never mentioned it because she was straight at the time and I felt embarrassed. She always had five adoring boys following her around, but they were never as important to her as her friends. Maria introduced me to Riot grrrl. It was her who took me to *Oh Bondage!* after a Fem Soc meeting one night. When we descended the stairs to the raucous shouts of Huggy Bear and the dancing drunken dykes and fags and neon lights and cigarette smoke I thought I'd found utopia. It got better. A grungy femme movie star in DMs and a prom dress smiled at me mischievously from the cloakroom. When you held my gaze for a gloriously long time, I felt a jolt of possibility. I miss that – I never feel it now, guess I'm too old. Maybe I've come to recognise that part of myself for what it is – the desire for something you can never have.

I was conscious of my bad dancing, my fit-like pogoing to Bikini Kill, my out of time steps to ESG. I looked at the floor when dancing with Maria. I expected you to find some reason to look busy when I came over to talk to you on a break from the dance floor, but alcohol made me brave. You mentioned you had a boyfriend and I went home that night cursing *yet another fucking straight girl*. Next month, when the boyfriend was gone, I practically hyperventilated with joy when you agreed to come to mine for a drink at the end of the night. Remember how we stayed up listening to records and talking, electricity building between us? It was turning light outside when our fingers brushed uncertainly against each other.

I never believed I could keep you. That thought was on my mind the whole year we went out. I was a useless, simple slob who didn't shut up, you were quiet and smart and intense. I know my inferiority complex drove you mad. I kept going on about how you couldn't possibly love me, wanting reassurance that would never be enough. I expected you to drop everything and everyone for me, got jealous when you looked like you were having a good time I was not the centre of, always accused you of wanting to leave me, which became a self-fulfilling prophecy. Remember how we went to see The Flaming Lips twice during our relationship, once at the start and once near the end? The first time was magical – that Technicolor music, those psychedelic lights, us holding hands, warm with whisky and love. The second time was one month after Elliot Smith stuck a knife into his own heart and my depression was getting worse. The Flaming Lips dedicated 'Waitin' for a Superman' to Elliot Smith, Wayne Coyne saying, 'If you don't know what it all means, that's OK, none of us know what it all means.' I started crying and you looked away.

'I just don't think I'm going to find anyone again. I mean none of us are getting any younger, are we?' I said to Maria. We were both sank into the sofa gulping cheap wine. We were twenty-one.

'No. But you will find someone again. And to be honest . . . I think you could do a lot better.' I don't know if you noticed Natalie, Maria never liked you. In my teenage arrogance I thought she just couldn't understand the intensity of being in love with a woman, that she would never get it.

'You know babe, I've always found Natalie to be a bit . . . stuck-up. A bit boring actually.' I knew why Maria was saying this – you came across as aloof because you didn't speak much and weren't socially outgoing like her. But that was just because you were so profound. 'When I'm talking she sometimes gives me this look, like I'm an idiot.'

My instinct was to protect you, Maria as well, to say, 'I'm sure that's not true', instead I found myself saying, 'Me too.'

'Then fuck her!' Maria gulped down the remainder of her wine and rose to her feet in one motion, grabbed her denim jacket covered in patches extolling the joy of feminist punk, abortion and communism. 'Come on babe, we're going out.'

Thank god for Maria. We didn't really have many big heart-to-hearts or anything, just sat next to each other, listening to The Bags or Peaches or Gravy Train!!!! or Siouxsie and The Banshees or Nirvana or Patti Smith or Bikini Kill. Sometimes she played me 7 inches by obscure Brazilian punk bands. But even Maria couldn't prevent my depression, always pushing at the door to my head, bursting forth and coming for me. I dropped out of university. You were not the cause, but I did think you could somehow fix me and that without you there was no hope.

It hurt when you told me you weren't coming to my leaving party before I went to London, you had other plans, but I swallowed it. *She's just a couple of hours away on the train*, I reassured myself, before you told me you were also moving, to Berlin. Always the optimist I prayed the move to another country would make you reflect on how much, unbeknown to you, you were still in love with me.

At the party I drank through the sadness like I always did. Me and Maria made cocktails that would probably kill us now and danced to X-Ray Spex, screaming along. Angry neighbours banged on all sides of our back-to-back terrace.

I remember you telling me how much you were enjoying Berlin the one time I came to visit, before spending the rest of the time recounting how awful it was. That the queer scene consisted largely of butches or trans guys or 'gender neutral' (almost always masculine) people, that as a femme you were often overlooked. That, trying to build allegiances outside the queer bubble, you'd joined an anti-racist reading group and got kicked out for expressing support for BDS, accused, mostly by gentiles, of being an anti-Semite.

Still, we had a ball. It was summer and we spent long days swimming in the lakes at the edge of the city, drinking in Görlitzer Park, watching German crusty punks and their gnarly dogs. We went dancing in a huge, shiny queer club one night and when I woke we were in an unfamiliar flat with four other naked queers.

We spent the whole next day in your bed, drinking Sekt and watching *Poirot* and *Midsomer Murders*, laughing as we tried to pre-empt the ridiculous plots. Despite our clumsy interactions at the orgy, our day in bed was platonic and I no longer wanted anything else.

Your Berlin flat was beautiful and you didn't work. Rent was cheap, you said. It *was* cheap, but I also knew by that point your family were loaded. Even after five years of being there you always spoke to service staff in English. Sometimes I'd ask how your German was going and you'd say it triggered your anxiety to talk about, so of course I had to drop the subject. It was beginning to dawn on me that you weren't actually a nice person. But was that important? We still had so much in common, and I hadn't laughed as much or been as happy the whole time I'd been in London as I was with you that summer.

Maria told me you were moving back to Yorkshire before you did. 'She's copying me! Well, she's only human. Maybe this means you'll actually visit now!' I had butterflies of nostalgia when I heard it was Hebden Bridge you were moving to. Though Maria had already lived there for two years, I associated it with you and the times we took the train there from Leeds when we were together. I still have photos of you sat by the canal, walking through the woods, necking wine by Sylvia Plath's grave. I'd been pretty shocked when Maria moved there. She'd always loved going out and seemed so at home in the city. I thought the Calder Valley must be kind of pathetic if you're from Brazil, but maybe you always think places far away are better. I know she and her girlfriend Christie got stares and outright hostility there at times, a dark-skinned immigrant and a trans woman in a small white town. Still, Maria told me the pros outweighed the cons: 'I'm old, I like the quiet, I like the country-side. I *love* my allotment. Any day now, I'm going to stop drinking!' I smirked when she told me that, thinking how twenty-one-year-old Maria would react to meeting this hippyish older version.

I was amazed to hear, during one of my phone calls with Maria, that she and you had become friends.

'I thought you didn't like her?'

'That was years ago! I was straight, you were a woman, we were all vegan.'

'Natalie's still vegan though, right?' You were one of the only people I knew who had never strayed from the animal-free path.

'Not anymore. She's gonna keep cows on the farm to sell organic meat.'

'What farm?'

'She's gonna buy a farm.'

'Wow! *Really?*'

'Yes. She's gonna employ people to work there.'

'She's gonna be a boss?'

'I think the idea is that it will be more of a co-op, even though she owns the building to begin with. And I'm gonna work there.'

'But . . . what about your job?' I thought she was having a breakdown. I couldn't believe she was just going to give up her career as a therapist to work on a farm for someone she'd always hated.

'I'm going down to half time. I'll help on the farm in the mornings. I need balance. If I just see clients all day I go crazy.'

I didn't know what to say to this.

'I'm excited, to finally have some queers in town.'

'Isn't Hebden full of queers?'

'Lesbians, babe. There's a difference. I thought I'd hit the jackpot, a town full of dykes, but they're all so wholesome and have these fucking women-born-women Christmas fairs. I'm just gonna be happy to have some friends in town who don't sit in judgement of me and my girlfriend.'

*

Maria is not a quitter, so the fact she lasted only a month at your farm was a bad sign. 'Babe, I would rather go back and work at my father's factory in Sao Paulo,' she told me in the deserted lesbian bar when I came to visit. Maria's father died of a heart attack in his forties, she always told me it was the factory that did it.

'Fuck. What did she do?'

'She slept in till midday while all of us were slaving from 6 a.m. She never lifted one of her fucking fingers, babe. It was shit, like we were her little maids. And she was always accusing us of stealing. Once, she came to my allotment on a Saturday and accused me of using her shovel to dig with and when I said, no, fuck off, I bought this shovel myself, she just sort of stood there watching me. I swear to god babe, it was creepy. I wanted to smash her over the head with that shovel. And she paid us less than minimum wage! Crying about how it's all she can afford, but she has so much fucking money from mummy and daddy.'

The bar lady, a dykey blonde approached us with excitement. 'Have you heard about the wall?'

'The WALL!' Maria's shouts reverberated through the empty bar. 'OH MY FUCKING GOD! The wall!'

'What's the wall?'

'I can't believe I forgot to tell you about the wall! Now that all her friend-slaves left, she's started thinking everyone's out to get her. She hired all these workmen to start building this crazy fucking wall around the farm. Oh my god babe, just wait till you see it!'

'You're going *inside*?' asked the bar woman, as though it were too good to be true.

'Yeah, I – I guess we're still friends.'

'Oh. Sorry . . . It's just your friend is a bit paranoid.'

'It seems so.'

'She doesn't come in here now,' the barmaid continued. 'She's fucked most people off too much. She tried to sell produce from her farm, but she was a complete nightmare to work with. Bad tempered, paranoid, such a control freak. Now she only goes to snooty places like Mildred's.'

Maria snorted. 'I bet she joins the golf club.' The two of them started cackling.

When I saw the farm, I knew you had lost it. I couldn't see the house itself, just the fields around it, the wilting crops and badly maintained fences, the skinny cows and the dilapidated barn and the monstrous wall. Black bricks stretching upwards, taller than the roof of the farmhouse within, surrounding it like a fortress. You came out through a heavy brown door followed by your frantic, vitamin D-starved cat and dogs, and waved a casual hello as though this was all normal.

'What's with the wall?'

'Oh, that? Just to keep the animals in.'

'Don't you think it's a bit big?'

'It's just nice to feel safe, you know? I'm alone up here and my experience of people has been pretty bad lately. Come inside.'

I was surprised how homely your farmhouse was, given what surrounded it. When we were having dinner and I asked you what you did up there all day, you were enraged and lectured me about how hard it was running a farm with no help, but I was just trying to understand how you coped. Same when I asked whether you saw many people and you reacted as though the question was a criticism and started going on about how all your old friends had abandoned you. It reminded me of when we went out and you asked about my coping strategies, and I told you I was clearly *not* coping and how dare you even ask.

'What's the wall *really* about?' was my last shot.

'Are you my therapist?' you sneered back.

I woke at midday. I'm usually an early riser but my body must have been confused by the lack of sunlight. I looked out of the window at the wall, thinking how lovely it would be if the daylight could stream in. Downstairs you were watching TV in your dressing gown, stroking one of your distressed-looking dogs. I was touched by the genuine affection you had for it, despite forcing it to live with you in this prison. 'I thought we could go to Mildred's for a late breakfast,' you said, showing no sign of tension from the previous night. 'I can run us down there in the car.'

'You know what? I need some air.' I felt oppressed by the darkness. 'I'm gonna walk, yeah? I'll meet you there.'

Then came the incident with the waitress and us parting ways forever. But before that, I left your compound, bolting the door behind me firmly as you'd instructed, so as not to allow the poor animals to see the sun. Hearing them scrambling at the door I felt like crying. I walked a hundred metres down the hill before looking back at the black fortress, a hellish dream.

My phone buzzed. Have you seen it babe? Did you get out alive? Pictures pictures pictures!

I read the message again. In it I saw all our futures. If she stayed, Maria would be the gossipy old hippie lady of the town, you would roam the fields with a shotgun, shooting at walkers who strayed too near the wall. And me, I would be somewhere else, trying to relive the first time I went to your house, the sunny cold day in Leeds, high on punk rock and the unstoppable desire of youth, wishing we could all go back.

Len Lukowski is a writer and performer living in Glasgow. He writes short stories, poetry, fiction, memoir and lyrics. He sometimes plays in queer punk bands.

Fluid – Isabel Costello

Today's the day, if it's ever going to be,
the day you hold me a second too long,
lifting us to another place.
The day when, instead of smiling down
as you kick through the leaves,
you smile up and ask
if I've ever thought how it would feel
to kiss you.

I say 'no',
because it's not a thought
or a wish, or even a dream
to touch the tenderest parts of you with mine.
It is more than any of those things.
You say you understand, but you don't
and nor do I, not really,
so we do it anyway.

As I watch the key tremble in your hand
there is only one way closer.
You are a different shape and yet the same,

round where I am lean,
chestnut to my coral.
Where I am, you are.
This is more than ache, thirst or desire
and it doesn't need a name.

Isabel Costello is the author of novels *Paris Mon Amour* and *Scent*, and her short fiction has been widely published. She is a creative writing mentor and tutor and has run the Literary Sofa blog since 2011. Isabel lives in London and has strong links with France.

Ten Years On – Kay Inckle

It was a moment before I recognised her. She was standing with some front-of-house staff as the last drizzle of theatre goers receded from the foyer. As usual, I had waited until last to leave. Otherwise, people kick my wheels and stumble over me in their hurry to depart whilst I pass unnoticed at waist height.

It was definitely her. Unmistakable, even though it must be ten years since I last saw her and, as well as being older, her hair was completely different. It was knotted into short tight stubs intricately spaced on her scalp. The last time I had seen her, the day I left the placement, her face had been framed by a huge halo of unruly black hair. But it was definitely still the same beautiful face: big, dark eyes, skin that looked like it was lit from underneath by the sunshine itself, cheekbones to die for, and wide, expressive mouth. She turned in my direction, I noticed she was wearing a lanyard. She worked here *and* she wasn't in front-of-house uniform. That meant she was doing OK, better than OK. My heart lifted. Something good had come out of that place at least.

Her eyes came to rest on me and I watched as, first a glimmer, and then a full smile of recognition spread across her face. I waited for the next bit: the inevitable look of pity as my transformation registered, followed by fear as the discomfort of having to talk to me took hold. But it didn't happen. Her smile simply deepened and she strode towards me with her characteristic vigour. She had always been athletic. She ran and played football even as a teenager when most of her peers had their faces stuck to screens twenty-four-seven. She was different, but that hadn't made her popular. Well, not with anyone except me. Her case notes had described her as surly and challenging, but even back then I was savvy enough to wonder if that was just because she was a smart, young black woman with big hair. And she definitely knew a lot more about the world than most of the staff, including me. Especially me. I had been naïve and full of white, middle-class confidence. But the scales had quickly dropped from my eyes. That's why I had left. I couldn't do it. I couldn't cope with trying to gaslight girls who were only a few years younger than me into lowering their expectations to the degree that staying off the streets and out of prison was considered a success. They were capable of so much more than that. They were worth so much more than that. That's why I was genuinely delighted to see Dayana working at The Lowry, doing well.

She looked like she was still sporty. She was wearing cropped, wide denim trousers, lace-up boots and a tight top that encased lean, sculpted curves. She came to a halt in front of me and for the first time she looked awkward. There is always awkwardness. But then she surprised me again. Her hesitation turned out to be just a moment of indecision about whether to offer me a formal handshake or a hug. In the end she leant down and wrapped her arms around me in a firm, warm embrace. She smelled of sweet, coconutty perfume. I could have held on to her all night.

'It's so good to see you Trish!' She beamed when she finally pulled back. She looked genuine, like she really meant it. 'I missed you so much when you left Northwest House, we all did. You were one of the good ones.'

'I missed you too.' Her warmth completely disarmed me and I was more open than we had been trained to be – even though that was ancient history now. We were supposed to cultivate clear, immovable boundaries. But I was rubbish at that. Even when I pretended to keep an emotional distance, I couldn't actually do it. It affected me too much: the cruelty and the suffering they had experienced and the injustice of it all. And I definitely couldn't keep my feelings about Dayana in check however hard I tried: the secret spark between us that felt divine and terrifying. I never told anyone about my feelings for her. I was petrified it would seem like I was some kind of predator, harbouring illicit intentions towards one of the girls I worked with. It was only later, when I was having counselling after my accident that I finally talked about it. It seemed so much more mundane then, in the cream-coloured counselling room. I liked one of the girls that I worked with. That was it. Nothing happened. She was seventeen and I was twenty. If we had met on a night out it would have all been perfectly fine and natural. It was just that we met in the half-way house where she was transitioning from care and I was a student on placement.

Counselling had made me think about all those boundaries again. Because it had sometimes felt more like we were supposed to maintain a line of privilege, or even pity, rather than emotional clarity between us. I was always acutely conscious of the rigid distinction between the staff and

171

students and the residents, despite the close proximity in age, the dress-down policy and the insistence on everyone using first names. Well, if it was a pity boundary, Dayana and I had definitely swapped sides of it now. All the white, middle-class privilege I had unabashedly occupied had disintegrated with the accident that bought me my wheels. Not the white bit, obviously, but my wheels stripped me of everything else. And *not* my wheels, I still sometimes have to remind myself; it's other people's reaction to them.

I had spent the first year after I came out of hospital avidly reading. It was one of the few things that I could do with the same thoughtless ease as before. So, whilst I had been trying to figure out what I could do with the rest of my life, I had started to give myself an alternative rehabilitation to the one that I got in hospital: a disability activism kind of rehab. That had also made me think about Northwest House again and the kinds of services that are imposed on the people we don't value. The intrusion and the control, like everyone else has a direct route inside you and yet there is no path beyond your current self.

'I wasn't cut out for social work,' I explained apologetically. 'I went back and changed my degree to sociology.' I felt a twinge of the old guilt at how easy my former life had been, and then I quickly added, 'What about you? What are you doing now?' I wanted to make sure she didn't get a chance to ask me about the more obvious changes. I hate it when people do that. Everywhere I go, which in fairness is not that many places, or certainly not the places I used to go given the lack of access, people seem to think they can demand that I explain my body to them. It humiliated and enraged me even before I could couch it in a language of oppression.

'I'm a lighting technician,' She beamed, 'I've been here eighteen months and I love it!' Her eyes swept around the glass, wood and concrete foyer, as if to check that it was enough to impress me. It was. She was. More than enough. Then her face clouded, 'Although there could do with being a few more faces like mine on the stage as well as behind the scenes.'

'I know,' I sighed, 'Change is painfully slow.'

Dayana looked at me and smiled again. Her eyes sparked. My stomach did a little somersault. That look in her eyes, surely it couldn't be ...? I pushed the thought away; she was just being nice. She was hardly going to look at me like *that* now was she? No one looked at me that way anymore. It was as if I had become completely sexless. 'What about you?' she asked, 'What are you doing these days?'

'I'm doing animation,' I said before I could think better of it. I had discovered and instantly fallen in love with digital animation on an arts course. 'I've done a couple of pieces for Dada Fest and some charities,' I rushed on, trying not to admit to myself that I was desperate to impress her. I normally avoid talking about it. I often have a strange feeling that if I get too confident before I have fully established myself it will jinx my chances of success. I don't know where I have got that idea from, I never used to be superstitious. I guess readjusting to my new place in the world where so much of my life is at the mercy of someone else's whim has made me less sure of everything.

'Can I see?' Dayana enthused, removing her phone from her back pocket. I gave her my web address and then I noticed the time. I really needed to start heading towards the tram if I was going to catch the train that I had booked the ramp assistance on. Even though pre-booking was no guarantee they would actually turn up, if I didn't get my scheduled service, they may well refuse the ramp altogether.

'I'm going to have to get my train,' I told her, anxiety about the potential pitfalls of my journey home momentarily overtaking my delight in seeing her again. Tram, train and then taxi for the last bit since my local station wasn't accessible and I wasn't going to risk the last bus crammed with pissed people making supposedly funny comments about my chair. There's only so many times you can smile politely when someone asks, 'Have you got a licence for that?' or if I have ever had a speeding ticket. It's amazing how much can go wrong in a journey that I once took for granted.

'Are you still in Liverpool?'

I was surprised, and pleased, that she had remembered. 'Yes', I replied wistfully. Every time I come to Manchester I felt the gulf of accessibility between the two cities. The tram makes a huge difference, but even some of the bars in the gay village in Manchester are wheelchair accessible. There's nothing like that in Liverpool. Not that bars were really my thing anymore. I have thought about moving. But it's too difficult – and not just the physical part of it. All the reregistering with different services, trying to get my benefits transferred from one area to another. And given the way the government uses any excuse to suspend people's payments it feels like too much of a risk. I keep telling myself it is something I will do when I am more established. Once I'm earning enough so that I'm not dependent on a vindictive state bureaucracy, then I will be free to live where I want.

'Are you getting the tram?' Dayana asked, and before I could answer, she added, 'I'll come with you. I'll just grab my things.' She darted off behind a 'Staff only' door and was back beside me with a jacket draped over her arm and a bag slung across her torso before I could fully acclimatise to what was happening. I had spent months after I left Northwest House fantasising about bumping into Dayana in circumstances where we could meet as peers, free from the structures of care and other peoples' judgment. I had wanted to be with her more than anything. But it was impossible. My dream of meeting her had never been fulfilled and, in time, someone else had taken her place in my heart. Well, until tonight, ten years on.

We passed through the automatic door. She moved easily at my side, her pace matching mine as we proceeded over the smooth slabs towards the tram stop. I was relieved she didn't offer to push me. I know people are only trying to be nice when they offer, but it still makes me feel like a sack of shit. I kept wondering when she was going to say something about my chair or ask me about the accident, but she didn't. She was watching another of my animations on her phone and she gasped and chuckled with pleasure as it played before her eyes. 'You're really good,' she smiled across at me, '*Really* good.' At the same moment a tram pulled into the platform ahead of us and we speeded up towards it. We were the last on board just before the doors closed. I angled myself into the wheelchair space, warm from the sprint. Dayana flipped down one of the folding seats and perched beside me, our knees hovering dangerously close together. 'I have to change in two stops,' she informed me, 'But how about we catch up properly soon?'

My heart lurched with such ferocity that I struggled to reply, 'Y-yes, yes, that would be great!' I hoped I didn't sound too shocked or desperate. The tram had already slowed to a halt again and a few people alighted into the inky night.

'I'll give you my number,' she said, taking control of the situation with a confidence and ease that I did not have a hope of matching. I rummaged in the pouch under my chair and pulled out my battered Samsung and tapped her number into it. The tram was slowing down again, this was her stop. She squeezed my wrist and stood up. 'It's really good to see you,' she said, searching my face with her eyes. I could only dream of what she hoped to find there.

'You too,' I replied, my tone as composed as I could manage. Then I panicked that I might have made myself sound disinterested, so I added with feeling, 'Seeing you again has made my night.' Dayana grinned and there was that spark in her eyes again. It made me want to reach up and pull her face to mine, to kiss her, and to not let her go. But I didn't. I simply watched her stride onto the platform, the imprint of her fingers dancing on my skin, my heart wringing itself in knots. She stopped and turned around, her gaze fixed on mine through the spattered window.

She raised her flattened palm to the side of her face. 'Call me,' she mouthed as the tram eased away.

Kay Inckle lives in Liverpool with her feline companions Precious and Lovely. She is a social researcher with a number of non-fiction publications. She writes speculative and social realist fiction, teaches Pilates and works on environmental and disability rights issues. She is also a vegan, handcyclist, swimmer and knitter.

Some Shadows Glitter – Katlego Kai Kolanyane-Kesupile

I've spent a fair share of my time thinking about the first First Lady of Botswana. Her name was Ruth Khama, née Williams. She was a white woman who moved to the country of her lover's birth to build a family. I was born into this country decades later. She moved to Botswana when the whole world was ablaze with racist and colonial fury about the interracial affair she was involved in. She left the relative comfort of being in a country where more people looked like her than didn't – where they shared (some) common cultural and traditional practices.

She left a world that, on the surface, was the place she would have been met with the least resistance and had more freedoms, to fight alongside a man she felt her life would be unhappy without. I think about her often, because much of what you hear about her always places her in relation to her husband. It would appear that the story of Ruth Khama is the story of the consequences of falling in love with, and staying faithful to, a man. This makes her a shadow; and as a Black transwoman, I have an intimate relationship with being made a shadow in my own luminous life story.

Before we, transgender people, are seen as full people who can make choices about how our lives should unfold, we are already told that we are violating the rules – a right reserved for few. Before we can think of ourselves outside of what others think of themselves, we are coerced to find fault in our self-worth. That gender is a social construct is something that people keep remembering to forget. That racism places ownership of Black people's lives at everyone else's mercy is violently denied. That women are defined by how much they are not men, and then met with violence when they behave 'like men' is something generations of feminists keep exhuming. However, these artefacts exhumed from the ruins of shaking the foundations of patriarchies keep getting returned to sender – much to my envy as an African (still) wishing our peoples' stolen artefacts would be returned as swiftly. These enlightenments get sent back to the pits that those who hunt us for sport keep heaving the bodies of Black trans women into. Our dignity is always placed in juxtaposition to our running appointments with gravesites marked out for us in people's minds and mouths. Yet these shadows they'd make of us resist being flattened and disappeared into the dark.

The plight of the Black transwoman is to keep remembering that she is both the light that shines and the shadow that sweeps over the world at nightfall. The plight of the Black transwoman is to remember that she is the confluence of phenomena and cannot be broken into parts. We are the site of many wars, yet we are regularly denied the agency to bring peace. This is why they try to destroy us whole – while we are alive. When they are not trying to destroy us, they want to love us in the dark – unseen, snuggled between the shame they fail to unwrap themselves from and the fear that they'll be the reason the violence has come home to us.

'*They*' is many people. *They* is the preacher who says we are all made from love and the greatest testament is to love our neighours as we have been loved, but doesn't take up the fight against the hatred their peers incite at every turn. *They* is the childhood friend who dead-names you because it holds the key to all the memories they treasure. *They* is the potential lover who doesn't understand why you're so irresistible to them, and what that means about their own gender or sexuality. *They* is the employer that interviews you for the records but never as a candidate to fill the position. *They* is not the children in the neighbourhood who wave at you with beaming smiles while you take the bin out. *They* is not the immigration officer who checks your particulars and still lets you board the flight even if the country of your birth misidentifies you in its official records. The latter beings are the ones who make the world a place we want to belong in without fighting anyone. These are the people that make me think about what it must have been like to be Ruth in a country where some criminalized her love and forced their hatred on her because of what they expected to be the will of God. Yet she, seemingly, knew that it was only the peace she found within herself that could grant her permission to exist. Romantic love aside, she chose to love the place she had chosen as home. She chose to stay in this place even after her husband's death. This is what baffles me: how her legacy is still framed through a person who wasn't there for many years of her life in this country.

I look at this in fear that, even as very visible contemporary queer people, transgender Batswana are always at threat of being erased when our backs are turned or our bodies laid to rest. I fear that we will be relegated to the shadows of things we now speak of as hearsay, like reptilian guards of sacred sites. I fear that the records of our resilience and the examples of our boisterous spirits will be divorced from the stories this land will hold onto about moments that shaped its identity. I fear that we may not even make it into mythologies. Yet, much like I spend time thinking about a woman whose legacy is separated from the fact that she was the white mother of a Paramount Chief, wondering what she might have introduced to the practices of her chosen people that still persists today but isn't attributed to her influence, I know that there can never be a history of Botswana that would be pleasing to hear without mention of queer people. That even in the shadows of 'subjects not for children', the music we make, the poems we write, the students we teach will stand and testify to our presence. But how does this not look like eulogizing yourself while you live?

Ruth's husband is notoriously quoted as having said that 'a nation with no past is a lost nation.' With these words, he sought the trust of his people in his modern leadership as the first elected president. These words, pronounced while leading the country towards an unimagined future, are summoned today as forewarning against the growing stronghold modernity has on youth in Botswana, so they never forget what their people are made of. In a fire that ravaged their house in Ruretse, Ruth and her husband lost many personal records. Many of the personal records covered their lives as public figures. Many of these records could have formed the skeleton upon which the body of Ruth's story is built. Her garments could have influenced a

First Lady-esque style in modern day Botswana. Her diaries could have offered a peek into the mind of a British woman tasked with grooming royal African heirs; questions she grappled with about the role she played in the development of young women in her tribe; secrets she kept from her husband; jokes she shared with visiting dignitaries; worries she had due to being the first in a line of many First Ladies to come; the list is endless. Much more than these private records were lost in the fire.

However, unlike Ruth, the fires we face as transgender Batswana are alive and always being reignited when we are only allowed to be consumed for recreation, and never acknowledged for the contributions we are making to this developing national history. Our lives become as ephemeral as dust storms in the desert. The fault is ours as much as it is in the hands of our fellow Batswana, who fear that adding us to a collective past will dilute the roles so neatly carved out for gendered practices that keep people thinking we can be modern traditionalists. That we are seen as a threat to what the colonial powers failed to crush is a fallacy that is as colonial as the tea we offer guests. So, in a country that only grants women places outside of its history, the plight of the Black transwoman in Botswana is to relentlessly occupy the collective consciousness that would reject her presence in totality. The plight of the Black transwoman is to be a glittering shadow.

I have learned this through observation and experience. It is too simple to say we are seen, when the truth is that we are seen more by those who want to extract us from the land that birthed us. This is why the national history of Ruth Khama does not exist for young women and girls to learn and explore their place in this society which keeps digging tombs (prematurely) for them. I shudder to think what will be done to the legacies of transgender revolutionaries in a time when I am not alive, considering what has been done to the legacy of a woman who loved a man to the point of making herself an outsider for her entire adult life. *They* swallow her story whenever her name is summoned. *They* keep swallowing and swatting and digging whenever a trans woman like me marks herself present. All this to uphold a flimsy veneer.

Someday, someone will probably try to say of my story: 'She was the Black transwoman from a tiny African country who thought that because she was smart and knew whiteness, she could turn herself into a white woman if only she tried hard enough.' This would not be wrong, again, if you only care about the surface and not what lies within. I want the same justice I seek for Ruth. I am an African who bought into the idea that success is measured by how much you are revered – is this not why we keep talking about the firsts in any and every space? I am a transgender person who agonisingly researched how nuanced the term could be in order to locate myself in it – because my own language did not accommodate people like me and I simply existed, dutifully, waiting for a natural end. I am a Black person whose cultural capital had been about how I could stand out as the exception to the rule of racist, colonial, sexist and/ or classist impressions of people whose only fault was being born in skin that duets with the sun yet gets called beastly. I want a womanhood with all the nuance of being more than someone else's something-or-the-other.

I am saddened, sometimes, by the fact that I look at my life as endless and see a horizon lined with possible impossibilities. This makes me a dreamer. This casts me as a being that only makes sense when you can't see anything. This hurls me into the world of the imaginary – and I would dare to say that I was taught that in the world of pure imagination, everything is possible. I cannot know what a life of freedom (not as a consolation prize or the result of stunting others) feels like, but that is only because I have been part of an era where we started showing that this world is built on our joys as much as on our cracked skulls, stabbed backs and lynched necks. Even when we are no longer here, when we are the stuff of rich shadows, we will still be seen, felt and heard. Some shadows glitter because they can always find the infinite light. I hope that one day, not too far from this one, I too will occupy someone's thoughts as they wonder when my story came to be my own. There, I will continue to shine.

Katlego Kai Kolanyane-Kesupile is an international award-winning Cultural Architect and Development Practitioner from Botswana with imprints in education, communications and human rights. Her work centres on decoloniality, feminism and disability theory. Her writing ranges from contemporary critiques, creative work in poetry, music and theatre, and scholarly research. Katlego holds an MA in Human Rights, Culture and Social Justice from Goldsmiths University of London.

Going West – Harry F. Rey

1990

We left our old life quite suddenly one morning before dawn. We'd been working in a busy country hotel in Mildura at the top end of Victoria, until Dad shook me awake. 'Mon lad, get up,' he said with an unknown fear written plain over his face. I never asked why we had to go. I never did.

Like all those times before, I packed a solitary backpack, still dusty from the last time we moved, with a few clothes and things sixteen-year-olds have. He hurried around the office, clattering about and knocking things over. Not many minutes later we set off in silence and in darkness, abandoning the few other staff that had loyally served him, the trunk full of things I didn't know.

We drove straight out of town and crossed the state line into New South Wales just as the sun rose and began to bathe the bare brush of the land in early light. The lines on the map just a different perspective on the roads sprawling out across the flat earth. No other activity passed our truck all morning, but the occasional farmer or doctor's plane would cut low across the blue sky as we made our way north. When, by lunchtime, I dared to ask where we were headed, all he said was: 'Time to go, son. Nae bother in hummin' an' hawin' about the past now, is there?' In that broad Scots accent which he'd never been rid of, like the ghouls from his past.

We were out to find us a new place to work, he said. The rent there had been no good, or the water stopped working, or some other reason that wouldn't stand up to scrutiny. But we just had to drop in on a few friends dotted here and there around the outback, then we'd be in the clear. I wondered what mess he'd left behind this time.

In a way I knew why we had left: to get away from all the things I didn't know about. I tried my very hardest not to wonder, as I had for as long as I could remember. Our journey took us through the great tracks that cut through the bare land of the backcountry, the great Australian interior: home to travellers, criminals, and exiles.

Dad passed the time by telling me half-remembered stories of the land, or about great wars or what Bob Dylan was really singing about as we listened to tape after tape. I'd spent the year since I'd stopped school working in his hotel, but this time with him was like a second education. Despite it all, the man who'd come from less than nothing, raised in a rainy Scottish orphanage before being shipped off to Australia, had the world to teach me.

Over days we drove on through fields of yellowed earthy brush plains and billowing wheat farms around the top of New South Wales. We reached so far North that we even skirted the edge of the tropics in the wet and humid green of Queensland, and passed through whole towns of dirt roads and blackfellas in the Northern Territory. We drove endlessly, crossing the dog-eared map that I'd lie in the back of the truck and study, on forever towards the horizon before a town might suddenly grow out of the bare earth.

Those days laying out on the back seat, kept cool by the air blowing through the open windows, with my back to wherever the sun happened to be, I did little else but study the maps. I learned the highways, the names of all the places in the bush and the lines that connected them. It was an unrealized, unknown fear of being lost on a whole continent that kept me reading, kept me learning the names of all the places we had named in this land.

Our stops offered some punctured relief from the journey. But we'd never linger, and each stop was essentially the same. Dad would make some calls from a payphone while I picked up supplies and looked for new tapes from whatever shops existed, casually avoiding stares or conversations. I easily looked like any other farm boy travelling through the harsh land for some unknown purpose. My tanned skin, sun lightened hair covered in a broad felt cowboy hat and a keen interest in maps and cassette tapes meant I easily blended into every place without suspicion. It gave Dad all the time in the world to conduct whatever business had caused us to be here.

Sometimes we'd take our truck to a flat roofed house at the edge of the town and sit for hours until dark, before Dad would get out and enter the house all of a sudden. At first, he'd pull together some bullshit story about visiting an old friend as we passed through, but towns later he wouldn't bother, and I didn't ask. I knew there were no friends, not in this state or any other.

Our purpose was as implied as it was unspoken. We'd

pick up things from people, take them somewhere and drop them off with someone else. Back at the Mildura hotel, there was an evident but subtle truth that a shadow business carried on all around me, one I'd never wanted to know about, but which so evidently affected my life whether I knew why or not.

One afternoon, which slowly turned into purple dusk, a good month after we'd begun the backcountry trip, we arrived at a town called Ceduna. My hazy dozing left in an instant as the name of the rusty place located itself in my head. We'd reached one of the last outposts of man in the eastern side of the great Southern continent. Somewhere not so far away was the sea. I could almost smell it. The rocks and edges of South Australia clashing against the Southern Ocean, held together by the A1 road that ran west along the cliffs. Beyond us the sun set over a red, rocky callous earth. I looked out to the horizon that gave way to an infinite dreamtime desert, to The West.

Out there existed a land of green treed roads and feather-white beaches that frayed along a sunset ocean. The red sun that sank in front of us pointed the way. I realized what all those tales from Dylan meant; it was about the escape of the west. It was a different west, but in my mind, it was the same; it was freedom.

'Am gonnae drop you off next tae the bottle-o, all right? Wait for me there and I'll be back in a couple of hours.'

Tyres whirled up red dust and he sped away. There was no cricket oval to sit by or kids to watch. Just the open road. I kicked a rock that crumbled into a dirt clod, squeezed the twenty dollars in the back pocket of my cut-off denim shorts, and gazed around at the flat-roofed buildings. They were nestled to the side of the unpaved road as if afraid of being sucked into the desert by the great sandy monster. A breeze came in from somewhere and rustled the plants, perhaps from the ocean.

'Going west?'

I spun around in a flurry of sparkling red dust. The man chewed tobacco like the men I used to pull pints for back in the Mildura hotel. He wiped oily hands on dirty overalls then brushed his grizzled face, half-hidden under a frayed red baseball cap. I couldn't take my eyes off it, the cap. I'd never seen anything like it. The words *NY Yankees* were embroidered to the front in white stitching. I caught a glimpse of a metal clasp at the back. The visor perfectly rounded to shield his eyes from the sun. It wasn't something from Target, it was real. A genuine artefact from the great American dream.

'You deaf, mate?' Lips chapped from the sun twisted like he'd found an injured joey who didn't want to be helped, but soft blue eyes radiated some kindness to me.

'Waiting for my Dad. He'll be back in a few hours.'

'So you just gonna stand here?' He looked around the dusty road. I took a glance myself, but was afraid to ask whom I might bother. 'I got some coolies in the back. You can come help me with the truck. Standing round here a dingo'll get ya.' He gave a smoky laugh and clapped me on the shoulder.

I could do nothing but follow rubber boots as they scraped across the brush towards a tin-roofed workshop. The low-fi buzzing of bugs in still air soon joined by the sound of machines plugged into electricity and the hum of an old fridge.

I found a perch on top of a pile of giant tyres that gave me a side-peek to the road should Dad come back and wonder where I was. The truck with its hood popped took up most of the space in the confines of the open-ended shed. A closed door led to a connected house. I took another good look at the incredible red cap as he dived inside an eskie; even the back had a miniature Yankees logo stitched into it.

He must have been to America, I decided. He'd gone straight after high school. Probably with an older brother. They'd been to LA, then flown to New York for a few days, and right in the middle of Times Square, he'd gone and bought a red baseball cap. The kind worn by the young blond boys that hit balls with bats in tight leggings then took showers together.

He threw me a beer and we cracked them open together. Embarrassed, I wiped dribbles of it from my chin.

'Where did you get the hat?' I asked. He hooked one side of his mouth up in a quizzical smile, a brushy upper lip from an unshaved smack of dirty blond hair which blended into dirtier blond skin. His lip looked like it could turn into a growl or a laugh with only a flick of an eyebrow.

'America.' He said, placing his beer down and diving back into the open truck surgery.

I nearly spit more beer out my mouth. If I was right about that, what else might I have divined? Sometimes I wondered if I had psychic powers, maybe from my mother, whoever she'd been. I always knew when a bar fight was about to break out. I could smell the change in air. The way men looked at each other dropped like a storm approaching. The violence always bubbling under the surface just ready to froth up and spill all over everything. I felt their feelings often before they did.

'When were you there?'

'A long time ago.' His voice echoed from beneath the truck's hull. 'Before I took over this chop shop from my old man.' He came up for air and swallowed half the can in two great big gulps. A breezy interlude trundled over the brush and swept around under the tin roof, puncturing my lustful dreaming with the cold reality that night would come soon. 'What's your old man up to?'

The question was asked with the tone of underlying acceptance that men who leave their sons on dusty roads at the edge of great wildernesses were somehow up to no good.

'We're heading west.'

'To Perth?'

'I guess. To the sea, anyway.'

'Perth's nice. Quiet. Although not as quiet as here.' He glanced at me. I could feel his eyes running across the lines of my bare leg, tucked underneath me, my shorts perhaps now riding up a bit too much for polite company.

'Where'd you come from?' He now leaned against the truck, arms folded, inspecting me. A chill cut through my bones like a social worker had just entered the room, or I'd bumped into a teacher who asked why I didn't come to school no more.

'Victoria. The country.' I swallowed a gulp of beer.

'Miss it?'

I shrugged.

'Me and Dad get around.' The weight of his eyes lifted and he turned back to the truck.

'You know engines?'

'Uh, a bit.'

'Well get on over here and I'll show you what I'm doing.'

I hurried over, eager for the opportunity to stand just

a little too close. He did a double-take on me, but carried on pulling stuff from the underneath. He talked about the engine and I listened, nodding to most of the things I already knew. But every time he moved his arm I got a chance to rest against his hot skin. To smell the moisture emanating from him, the underlying musk of sweat and manly stuff.

I felt the night-time hunger that creeps up in the silence of my darkened room before I sleep. The great and terrible monster that watches over me, day and night, sometimes hidden, but always there, inside my head.

The monster has many faces. A boy at school some time ago in silky purple football shorts that barely contained his milk-white muscular thighs. The young truck driver who sat and drank in Mildura hotel on his way to and from places. I always rushed to refill his glass, living on the winks he shot me and the times he called me son. Or any number of anonymous faces and bodies who passed me by on their ways and wanders. Who let me sit and steal their images for the goings on inside my head. Un-abreast of my thoughts and unaware that I fed their toned and tanned bodies to the monster in my head.

*

'You're quiet.' Dad said to me as our truck shuddered along the night-time road, breaking the silent sound of darkness. 'Did that bloke gie you the hat?' I pulled the frayed red brim further down my face, tucking myself and my monstrous smiles from Dad's eyes.

'Yeah.'

'Good on him. Nice fella.' Dad said, now to himself.

'Sorry it took me a bit longer, son. But that's us all done now.'

I turned around in the seat, the brim of the hat pushing against the window and giving just the right amount of pressure against my neck to make it almost comfortable.

The lines of the road flashed into existence then out into nothing, illuminated by the presence of our headlights. If we had not been here to bring the light, would there be any road at all? Did it actually exist, this line in the map, a thousand miles long, or was it simply laid out before us because we decided to travel on it? Part of me wondered if there was really any west at all. I'd never seen it. Only the sun rising in the east then setting over mountains and desert. Only my Dad and maps told me it was real. And one of them lied to me. One lied all the time.

'We'll get some good grub tomorrow, all right? First thing. In a few days we'll be there. You'll like it, I know you will. A real beach, warm sand, endless ocean.'

This time the monster that came at night felt different. Less like a monster, more like a friend. A friend who once gave me beer, and who I helped with his truck while my Dad was gone for hours and hours. A friend who all at once made the monster real, but showed me there was nothing to be afraid of. Monsters made you feel bad, not good, and I felt so good. Monster's didn't hug you tightly afterwards, kiss you on the cheek and give you their favourite hat they'd brought all the way from Times Square.

'I'm telling you son, things are better out west.'

Maybe this lost old man was on to something. I wasn't lost, just unfound in unfamiliar surroundings. Going west meant going into the unknown. Not as me anymore, now I'd shed the virgin skin of a child. Now I had a token from someone else. My existence had been seen, acknowledged, desired. I'd been crowned with a lover's gift. I was no more imaginary lines on a dog-eared map, or the watcher in the shadow. I wasn't lost, just undiscovered. Yet with the first inklings of the body of land I could be. Now, going west, I could be real.

Harry F. Rey is a Scottish author of LGBTQ fiction. His works include the gay rom-com *All The Lovers*, the royal romantic drama *The Line of Succession* and the queer sci-fi series *The Galactic Captains*. His new historical novel, *Why in Paris?*, will be published in 2022. @Harry_F_Rey

CBeebies Has a Lot to Answer For – Victoria Richards

She asks questions you wouldn't think of asking, like *How do you make a bouncy castle?*
How cold is the ice on an ice rink? How does a toilet flush?
Sometimes she scrunches up her eyes like she's seen a magpie
making love in a nest of razor blades, sometimes her yellow hair reminds me of a noose –

Maddie Moate won a BAFTA for her work hunting pre-historic shark teeth, for teaching kids about bones and the world's largest, smelliest flower. She even went to Bali for a month just to find out how rice grows.

Maddie, Maddie Moate: for you I'd write poetry with wax crayons from the factory you showed us in series one, scrawl sonnets across the walls of an old church.
I'd hide love-letters in cans of beans and throw them out to sea

*

for sharks with tin-opener teeth to swallow whole until they rattle
deep inside a child's nightmares, because they watched *Jaws*
when they weren't supposed to, because it was the seventies
and red-froth blood didn't hurt as much thirty years ago.

Maddie Moate – *the woman I love/am in love with –*
has had a terrible time with her skin (I watched her vlog
about it). Sometimes it flares up so badly she has to spend
five hours in make-up

just to be able to say 'I love the way he paints a monkey on
the plastic, don't you?' while
bouncing up and down on fifty sheets of rainbow-coloured
polyvinyl.
I once tweeted her to ask where she got her amazing red
trainers

but she didn't reply, and I felt like getting myself lost in the
nearest desert just so they'd do a TV report about me, just
so she'd notice,
but I've never been very good at practical things like survival

or saying what I want (or don't want) or putting Ikea furniture together. I once made a chair and screwed all three
legs on upside-down
I once thought about using the train tracks as a pillow –

I am in love with a woman who doesn't know I exist and
sometimes I don't know if I do.
Do You Know? Let's Find Out

Victoria Richards is a London-based journalist. A collection of her poetry was published in May 2019 in *Primers: Volume Four*, with Nine Arches Press, and in 2020 she came first in the 'Nature in the Air' poetry competition and second in the Magma Poetry Competition. Find her @nakedvix

Camp at the Grocery Store – Claire Orrange

Last night I dreamt I went to the grocery again. When I woke up, so electrified was I, and so depleted was my kitchen, that it was hardly a hop, skip, or jump to the conclusion that today was the day. Saturated as my mind is with early 2000s movie montages of shopping-sprees and makeovers, the outing decidedly became a project of passion and conscientiousness; the grocery store was my mousey and hunched muse of a new girl, just awaiting to fit in with me, the most popular girl in school.

I'm kidding, of course. I want to get down to business because I'm rather scatter-brained and this story requires a laser focus. I once read an op-ed in the newspaper (checking the hubris I had had that told me that print journalism was dead, having been killed by the internet star) about a man who was arrested for shining a laser pointer at a plane in an attempt to distract or blind the pilot and send the contraption hurtling into the ground. It was titled 'The Perils of Democratized Technology in a Post-9/11 America.' I liked the accompanying picture:

a digital rendering of a puffy blue sky with clouds in the shape of weapons.

But I digress and digress and the grocery story idles. I suppose one could say that my mind makes an arbitrary choice at each moment to either sustain an unnecessary amount of focus on something or to wander off and play with the information of the world that dances around like the sparkling stars that appear at the periphery of one's vision when one stands up too fast. Shrewd is not my middle name.

I surveyed my pantry and refrigerator (childish letter magnets on its steel veneer read *WERE ALL BORN NAKD . . .*) and eventually coalesced these observations into a shopping list. From there I took my time in assuming my outerwear and shoes. Taking pleasure in this process is a woman's prerogative after all, as is tending to the garden and sipping cherry cola. It was a sunny day, and the sprinklers were going, so I indulged myself with a romp through the yard. My clothes were rather soaked by the time I was through, but I didn't mind. Smoke cut through the droplets of water and rose towards the sun as I summoned the mental defences necessary for an outing on-the-town.

My driving has never been stellar, in fact I'm sure it has set women back several years here and there. Long ago, I almost hit a child foolishly chasing her beach ball onto the steaming pavement while I was listening to Tracy Chapman. I almost wish I *had* hit her, if only to fulfil the prophecy laid out by driver's license tests which proclaim that children chasing balls into streets are a public health emergency (along with cannabis). With time, however, I became more and more grateful that I had not, as taking on the baggage associated with vehicular manslaughter of an innocent child is so trite, and forward, forward I must go.

Which brings me back to the grocery store. How accurately the list reflected the actual needs of the household, or how I ended up in the parking lot with my reusable plastic bags (the oxymoron is not lost on me) on that balmy day are both not clear to my recollection. Nonetheless, the shopping list told me to buy five eggs. To my dismay, the grocery store sold eggs in Styrofoam bouquets of six and twelve, positively nuptial. I frowned and thought. My face was illuminated by the fluorescent light, rendering the rows of Styrofoam shiny and pastel. My wandering mind's eye was recalled to an image of a golden hen sitting on a perfectly circular, cartoonish nest. Was it a farmer who tenderly retrieved her egg and shipped it off to some global supply chain? I didn't like the contrast of sterile dazzling eggs here and the farmer tending to the fowl mother up there, up in my thoughts.

I must have been stuck in that position, scowling down at the eggs, trance-like, for a while. I kept seeing the supposed farmer, a snapshot of gingham and worn hands, and the chicken, proud and demure, doing their egg dance, on a loop. In an attempt to join in on the hypnosis, to answer the chicken and the egg (and the farmer), I slowly picked up a half-dozen carton. Staying in beat, I put it in my cart. Only, that wouldn't do, because the list called for five. The idea to take an egg out and put it back struck me as a means of release. I did so. I hid it behind a carton on the top shelf.

I heaved a sigh of relief. 'Next, broccoli. If only I could simply speak the broccoli into existence in my shopping cart. I'm not a witch and yet – '

'I'm sorry, are you Susie's mom?'

I turned to my left, noting broccoli was to the right, and faced the woman posing the question. She looked vaguely familiar, but the likelihood that I had simply seen her in the parking lot or next to the pyramid of chicken noodle soup cans at the store's entrance was sufficient to stop me from venturing a guess at our connection. Can't *poof* that one into existence either, I half-smiled.

'No, not Susie's mother, I'm sorry, she's brunette after all, I'm remembering now, but surely we know each other? You look so familiar.' She blinked her big eyes. They had that look of sleep deprivation, like the skin laying over her orbital bone had been tanned, and the veins were rivers of runoff from the industry. I might have told her this, given that I lack a key filter somewhere between the mysterious origin point of all of my thoughts and my traitorous tongue, but, all things considered, was it not likely that her husband or father or grandfather, if not all three, had lost their factory jobs years ago, and my words would have only served to surface that repressed memory from the musty annals of her mind?

This hesitation on my part gave her mental acuities far too much credit, I'm afraid. Instead, my grin turned into a strained smile, which struck me as appropriate given that directly behind this woman was a glossy sign directing me to the *cheese* section. 'I get that a lot. Must have one of those faces. Maybe you saw me in a dream.'

She didn't seem to be listening. I contemplated the absurdity of her decision, to confront a stranger with questions in all earnestness, only to ignore the response. I could not make sense of this woman.

'Say, you're not Gabriel Carmen's wife?'

My nostrils must have flared. The broccoli would become rot and sand at this rate. For, indeed, Gabriel Carmen is my husband, but hearing his full name in this manner only served to make me think for the millionth time that pleasant words, like *Gabriel* and *Carmen*, strung together and spoken aloud sound like the identity assumed by a porn star. Can words be aphrodisiacs?

> *Carmen, Carmen.*
> *The words themselves disarmin'.*
> *Can't be any harm in*
> *Farmin' his—*

'Wife?' Her inquiry caught me by surprise and tipped the fulcrum of my perception. I was assaulted by the lurid display of colours, which, my laser-focus on five eggs and broccoli hindered as it were, suddenly revealed itself to me in a grotesque vision of the psychology of advertising. Reds demanded immediate attention, but yellows and pinks were more pleasing to the eye, and of course greens evoked nature, and – my eyes must have wandered off – to say the least, my unnamed inquirer conjured my attention back to her sleepy eyes.

'Yes, of course!' I heard the exclamation point. 'My, you're one lucky lady. He's quite a – only you know all this of course. Gee, I bet you get women like me coming right up to you all the time, with a husband like that.' Her interjections of *say* and *gee* were that of a girl at the malt-and-drug store on her date with the dreamboat quarterback. She had a ribbon in her hair, to complete the caricature.

'You're very sweet. So, we must have met at the …?'

'… we met at Mark's wedding.' She nodded with satisfaction, as though landing on her relation to me consummated these wasted moments.

'Oh.' But then again, she was so perfectly placed here. Her earnest outfit of button-up top and maxi skirt was assembled together in a Frankenstein of a 'look.' I would have been recalled to some term or another I learned in college about the wholeness and contentedness that is felt when subject and environment are in perfect alignment. I would have again thought about the warm hearth in which the farmer cooks the eggs drawn from the plump, knowing hen. But she looked so expectant, like a dog that has performed a trick and is waiting for a treat, that the 'Yes, he is my brother. Are you a friend of his husband?' came out begrudgingly, and thoughts of such associative nature were not given their proper due.

She beamed. 'Are you kidding? Remy is, like, totally my gay best friend. Ha!'

And there the illusion lay in tatters before me. She rambled on and on, interpreting my clipped replies as merely opportunities for a full breath before continuing. I considered and finally decided to cut her off and attend my date with the broccoli when her itinerant monologue took a turn for the political, although qualifying it as such is a stretch. I should not have been surprised that she praised the president's leadership qualities, and the unprecedented nature of his election, if not his 'shaky' handle on policy. I should not have been surprised that she normally did not concern herself with that sort of thing, and anyway, her husband told her who to vote for. At last, what could I do but humour her?

'Gabe is planning to purchase a gun to shoot the president, I believe.'

She gulped and her lower lip began to quiver. I immediately regretted upsetting the placation into which she had allowed herself to recede during the course of our meeting. She was like the baby that is awoken from its slumber to find its father rocking it back and forth since its bitch of a mother won't give him any affection, and after a long day at work he was entitled to some human contact. She was like a housewife, tending her garden, confronted with Sally next door wearing blue jeans while breastfeeding in the openness of her front porch. In short, she made a hurried goodbye. I wondered if the Gabriel I let slip jived with the Carmen that she appropriated in order to first initiate our conversation. Can words be aphrodisiacs?

The nameless woman, for I could not recall our drunken introduction at my brother's wedding, replaced the chicken farmer and egg up there and assumed the throne of contemplation. Perhaps she had something worth emulating, embodying the sheep that defines the 21st-century just as perfectly as the listless cigarette smoker did the previous. I do not know why I find myself so *boggled* at real Americans, although, do not let me be misunderstood, politics hardly interests me either. Remembering those moments in the grocery store leaves me with this agitated feeling of jealousy. Gabriel ought to have married a woman like *that*. But I ramble when I should be blunt: the haze produced by the abundance of drugs I consumed this morning of my retelling, as indeed that particular morning as well, led me to omit, in my own assessment of the events of that day, the critical importance of my effeminacy to the fallout of events. It is something Gabriel absolutely insists I do not linger on, and I wish I could say his dominion over my material life eventually sequestered the deviance to some sort of haven within my mind, where it has had free reign, *Pax Trannica*, but he has permeated that too. He always used to say that his love for me was 'funny but regrettable ...' (his trailing off, not mine).

However, having set out to tell this tale it behooves me to move along, move along. As it turns out, the natural colours and textures of the produce section exercised just as much control over my limited faculties as Miss Falling America and all of the advertisements had previously. How could I resist the alluring glow of a yellow bell pepper? I hid a hairy kiwi in the Styrofoam hollow meant for the sixth egg. I ate a bushel of red grapes right then and there, arousing some consternation among the other shoppers. But these organic conceits paled in comparison to the broccoli that I had so lusted after. 'It's a power trip,' I proclaimed to no one in particular as I examined the tiny little trees that I could purchase and consume at will, which looked like some microcosm of biopolitics and deforestation. Gabriel was on a work trip which, for all intents and purposes, meant that I had an infinite extension to my leash, and the possibilities therein were almost as tantalizing as the political dimensions of all of this shopping.

Farm hen, Big ben.
Swimming mermen.
Vit-a-min Season.
The Sword and the Sheep (Pen).

And so on. The broccoli lit a fuse that culminated in an explosion of consumerism. I decided that the chicken noodle soup pyramid just *had* to be excavated for its bounty. I could not resist the Devil's Food cake (situated next to her sister, Black Forest) and nearly destroyed its delicate icing pattern by tossing it into my shopping cart.

The chips! Baked, broiled, and beautiful. I snatched the last of some colourful candy or other out of the hands of a small child. I *hooray*'d the presence of sugarless protein bars. One of the workers, demarcated by her glossy visor, eyed me warily, but I felt all the more encouraged by her silent judgement.

My cart was brimming with these treasured contents by the time I wheeled my way to the final aisle waiting to be deflowered by my presence: that of the *frozen*. TV dinners never fail to make me laugh out loud. I would have loved to introduce my assailant-by-the-eggs to her perfect match, her ideal conversationalist: the sad weight loss system meal. I threw five into the cart.

If this country is all about coming and going and roading and whoring and shooting and booting then I should not have been surprised that I, with appropriate smoke and mirrors, all at once made my way to the checkout as though the frozen food aisle I left behind hid all of my darkest secrets, and I was running out of time.

'I've got to get back on that open road.' I smiled at the stout, pimpled cashier who stared vacantly back at me. I would have begun following some psychic thread about the nature of teenage inertia if, from behind, I didn't hear, 'You make a cute Kerouac.'

It was Gabriel. I landed a punch to the side of his arm for startling me. We made love with our eyes as the broccoli and eggs (and sneaky kiwi) were scanned into my bags. We proclaimed the renewal of our toxic marriage right then and there. He bought all of the groceries with cash in a nostalgic homage to our first few dates at local restaurants, in which we both wore sunglasses indoors so as to not bring about his identification or mine, our honeymoon phase.

But of course, none of that happened. In fact, the trans-action was never completed, for, all at once, everyone in the store was alerted to an 'emergency situation develop-ing in the parking lot' over the intercom, and, starved for excitement as suburbanites are, nearly everyone ran outside, including my feckless cashier.

How would the headline of the news report capturing that day read? 'Car Bursts into Flames at Local Grocery Store; Will America Rise from Its Ashes?' in which the author thinks not; or maybe 'Area Woman Less than Distraught by "Cleansing" Car Fire'; 'Prominent Politician's Wife Basks in the Glow of Dante's Sedan' etc. etc. In truth I felt a remarkable ease settle over my body in the ensuing moments. No innocent people were hurt, not even the inhabitants of the next car over. It was my pig's blood prom moment, sweltering in the heated ripples of the Obama administration. Shortly thereafter, Gabriel ran for re-election and lost to a woman, around my age, whose fake tan was almost as obvious as her selling out to the argi-business lobby. We became fast friends.

And that, I suppose, is what I've been trying to say. Camp at the grocery store is the perfect subject and setting because where else is there as much dissonance between thing promised and thing gained? Shiny soup can; luke-warm broth. Amusing woman; dangerously apathetic. The open road; death by fire. The golden years of progress; the gilded years of precipice. It's *naïveté*; it's the USA.

Claire Orrange (she/they) is an American writer and junior at Harvard University studying history and literature. She enjoys gardening and performing stand-up comedy, and splits her time between Boston, Massachusetts and Buffalo, New York.

Just Coming Home – Rosanna McGlone

Listen. Can you hear that? It's the waves. I'm going through the water. (Sighs). It's been a long journey, so it has.

I've got to get out on the deck, before it's too late. God, it's Baltic up here. I need to hap up. Flecks of sea spray lick my cheeks. I stick out my tongue to taste the saltiness, a wee girl appears from nowhere, pointing and giggling and tugging her mammy's arm. In the distance I can see the Tower, orange bleeding across the sky. Go on, have a wee hoak.

I cudden 'a' done this any other way. It wouldn't have been right. A plane gets you places, aye, but this time it's not just the arrival, it's the journey. And it's been a long journey, I can tell you.

I've left my mammy and Plunkett and Maureen and Mickey and Lucia and wee Bernadette back in Dromore. What time is it? Aye, Mammy'll be up by now, the cows need milking, so they do. She'll mebbe have seen the envelope, but she wudden 'a' opened it yet. Then she'll be going up to St Dympna's for morning mass.

I was an altar boy there, you know. Every Sunday

211

eleven o'clock sharp I was there on my knees, prostrating myself before Jesus and the Virgin Mary and God knows how many statues, and back again at five for benediction, swinging my incense like there was no tomorrow. (Beat) And now there won't be, not for me. Not at St Dympna's, that's for sure, nor any Catholic church. When I get off this boat, everything's going to change. In my head, it already has.

So why now? Daddy died last May. An aneurism. If it sounds sudden, it's because it was. One minute he was in his armchair cheering Ballymena, they were thrashing the Crusaders so they were, the next he was slumped with his head back. Mammy shook him and shook him, but he was dead. It was desperate. Ballymena lost. Don't get me wrong, I loved me daddy, but he was like a wee bag of weasels, so he was. And if he'd ever thought I wasn't his big lad he'd a decked me one, right enough. I could never have done this if he'd been alive.

It started, perhaps, when I was nine. Mammy and Daddy were out visiting Uncle Jimmy's place. We'd been sent home from choir early as Mr Gilligan had fallen sick. I crept into Maureen and Lucia's wee room and sat at the dressing table. There were lots of bits of make-up scattered across the dressing table. Stuff Auntie Emer had given to Maureen when they were nearly finished. Mammy didn't approve, but what could she do? Everyone loved Auntie Emer, and no one could say no to her.

At first I just sat there, dazed. It was like I was in a sweetie shop, only the shopkeeper had gone home, so he had. I stared at them in wonderment: Bubblegum Pink; Plumful; Sateen Promise; Burnished Bronze; Shy Time Shimmer.

I reached out for one: Pink Candy. I sat there with it in

my hand, feeling the smooth tube, rounded like a bullet, just holding it in my warm palm like me daddy held a pint.

And then, then I took off the end and raised it to my lips. I had to twist it really, far round to find the tiny, pink nub sticking out like some rude temptation. And temptation it was. I felt like Jesus in the desert, only without his willpower. The stool was wonky and I'd no idea, that first time, what I was doing. I was so scared, my hand was shaking so it looked pretty wobbly, but I tell you, when I looked at myself in the mirror, it felt fantastic!

The next time, I went a step further, so I did. I tried on our Maureen's bra. I touched my breast beneath the soft, white cotton. My body tingled as if a huge current was coursing through me. For the first time in my life, I felt alive. I was terrified though that someone would catch me and then I'd be dead. But they never did. It became a habit. Every Saturday when everyone was out, I'd slip into the girls' room and live.

Why have you waited so long? That's what you're thinking, isn't it? I found the clinic on the internet four years ago and I've been saving up ever since. Nearly 20,000 pounds's a lot of money. When Daddy died I was still £9,000 short. And then they read the will. 'And to Dermot, I leave one sixth of the farm ... and £10,000.'

So here I am, traiking across the water, like some almighty birth canal, so it is. Look at these big hands of mine. I'm not sure they'll be able to change those, but the rest of me ... aye, they'll change enough on the outside.

It's been a rebirth alright. They'll change me on the outside, but you know, it'll still be me on the inside, the same Dermot as I've always been. Wherever you are, this is me, Daddy. Oh God, Daddy, ya never understood, but nothing's changed, not really. The only thing that's really changed is yous. I'm hoping Mammy and the girls and Plunkett will forgive me. That one day they'll understand and there'll be no more pretending, so there won't.

Did you hear that? The ferry's shuddered to a halt, and I'm standing here on the deck looking out at my new life. My eyes are shining. Jeez, I cudden 'a' done this in Dromore, and not because there's no clinic either. I've been waiting my whole life for this. This is who I am, right enough. So you see, I'm not really leaving, I'm coming home, so I am, I'm just coming home.

Rosanna McGlone is a journalist, writer and biographer who has been published in England, Australia and America. Her work has appeared in the *Guardian*, the *Independent* and the *Australian*. She loves chocolate, Italy and her family Quin, Octavia and A.B. https://www.facebook.com/RosannaMcGlone

The Beautiful Ones – Nathan Evans

As the curtain comes down, Steven checks the mirror behind the bar, smooths side-swiped hair, swabs stray mascara, and tries to ignore the bowtie the theatre makes him wear. The audience clap, obscuring the exit music; never one to miss a zeitgeist opportunity, Tom has gone for 'Beautiful Ones', its brazen optimism seeming to soundtrack their times: soon there would be a new government.

And there he is as the lights come up again, the man of the moment: not beautiful, but handsome in that tux he's wearing, Tom steps from the baby grand, smiling as his nostrils catch the sweet smell of press night success. His eyes catch Steven's, and Steven is smiling so hard it's hurting; that man up there is his man.

Then Tom's eyes move on: the maestro has been joined by his star. Julie is the beautiful one. Blooms that magically match her gown have materialised in her hands. The audience start whooping, and soon will be swooping on the bar for the free wine Steven has laid out for them.

By the time all the reviewers have been replenished at least once – most often more – and air-kissed out the door by

Dougie, the producer, by the time all their glasses have been rallied and rinsed and racked, Steven fears the party will be over. But it sounds like they're still high-wired.

He knocks, adopts a nonchalant stance. 'Come in!' Dougie's voice comes back at him, his words with always at least one extra syllable in them. As Steven codes the door open, Dougie's pouring champagne. 'Darling, you're just in time!' He slips a flute into Steven's hand.

'And then this cock comes through the cubicle wall!' Tom is full-flow across the dressing room. In light less flattering, his hair is thinning. Tux on a railing, he's changing into something more casual and taking the opportunity to casually show his pectorals.

'No!' Julie is playing straight man, though she's actually a chain-smoking lounge-singing lesbian – lipstick now counterpointed by boots and jeans. It had been Dougie's idea to partner her with Tom for a postmodern reinvention of popular songs. It seems to be working.

Tom holds his hands pec-width to indicate the length of said appendage. 'I'm not kidding.' He's trowelling on his thickest Yorkshire accent.

'Darling, do stop bragging.' Dougie refills their glasses. 'There are children present.' They like to remind Steven of the age difference: Tom is seven years older than him. He was a visiting lecturer at drama college; Steven had been smitten and seduced in his final term. Then Tom got him the bar job on graduation.

Julie smiles sweetly-slash-smugly. 'Isn't he handsome in his uniform?' Her vowels are purest Essex. Steven feels himself flush the colour of his waistcoat.

'The lesbian's for turning.' The man of the moment knows girls who do boys like they're girls are all the fashion.

'Stick to the curtains, darling. Men are all beasts.' Not for the first time, Dougie flutters his eyelashes in Steven's direction. 'Present company excepted.'

'Cheers!'

'Cheers!'

'Cheers!'

'Well done.' Of course, Steven had loved it.

'So, you liked it?' But Tom doesn't need to be told that.

'I did.' Steven has to maintain *some* power in this relationship.

'That's all we're getting, obviously.' Tom swings the spotlight back his own way. 'Where was I?'

Julie is cued and ready. 'The cock was coming through the cubicle wall, I believe!'

As they slip back into their routine, Dougie sidles up to Steven. 'You don't get jealous?'

Steven had worked out that monogamy wasn't going to work for him before he'd worked out he was gay, even: he couldn't give a shit how many 'cottages' his boyfriend frequents. He shrugs. 'It's less for me to deal with.'

Steven is woken by a hand panning down his body. Last night they'd drunk too much to get anything up, so Tom has woken horny. Tom is *always* horny. Steven rarely initiates sex, for fear of risking rejection, but rarely resists when it's offered him. That too is risky, without a condom, but Tom had been insistent. They'd been seeing each other almost a year when Steven had surrendered. He's pretty certain that, with the others, a hand-job is as far as Tom ventures.

'That's better.' Tom spoons closer.

Now it's over, Steven needs him out of there. 'Is it OK?'

'Bit pooey.'

Steven is on the toilet doing the necessary when Tom – never one for boundaries – squeezes by. 'I feel like shit.'

'Yeah, you look it.'

'Ta.' Tom seeks a second opinion in the Habitat mirror: his bathroom may be bijou, but the decor is impeccable.

'What time is it?'

'About eleven.'

'Better get moving. Got an audition.' Another advertisement: nothing exciting. But he's still not had a gig since graduation and the pay is handsome. 'What you doing?'

'Lying in the recovery position. See you after the show then?'

'I think I might stay at mine,' Steven says, flushing.

He spends most of his time at Tom's place, but has his own when he needs space. By the time the show comes down, the appeal of retreating alone to 'bedsitland' has waned somewhat, so he decides to try his luck on cuddles and cock. He knocks at the dressing room door. No answer, no one there. Wilting flowers top-scent the air. Tom's tux adds a bass note: Steven inhales his man in absentia.

'Where are you?' He can hear Tom's in a bar – gay by the sound of the Kylie.

'Went for a drink with Julie.'

'Oh.' Steven shoulders the still-new mobile to his ear.

'Didn't say you were coming so . . .'

'Shall I come join you?' Steven leaves through stage door.

'You could do . . .' Which means *no*. 'But we're both feeling a bit post-press night. I think we'll just have one and turn in.'

Steven finds himself feeling rejected, and dejected by the prospect of a night in his single bed. 'Alright,' he compensates. 'I'm not on tomorrow night so I'll make some food for when you get back.'

He's had a key since leaving drama school: he'd stayed at Tom's place in Notting Hill while scouring *Loot* for something vaguely affordable within a square mile. He puts down his shopping, peddle-bins his gum. And spots the butt beside his foot. Tom doesn't smoke, neither does Steven. The plot thickens. On closer inspection, the butt exhibits a trace of scarlet lipstick. The bass drops.

When the door opens, Tom's favourite *Piano Man* is on the Bang & Olufsen, the wine is open and – with more energy than may be strictly necessary – Steven is grating parmesan.

'Hello! How was the show?'

He surprises Tom with a kiss, isn't usually so demonstrative. He expresses affection more readily through the medium of cookery: he's made his boyfriend's favourite linguine.

'Storming. How was your audition?'

'That was yesterday.'

'Oh. Sorry.'

'Not heard anything.' Not yet daring to dig into that cigarette end's origins, Steven digs pasta from the pan.

Tom goes straight for the wine. And to the heart of the affair. 'Listen . . . Last night, Julie came back.'

'I know! She left her fag butt!' Steven turns his voice up to full brightness.

Tom seems disarmed by this, fortifies himself for whatever comes next. 'We ended up having sex.'

A million disconcerting emotions pass through Steven as he passes the pasta from pan to plate. He permits Tom to see none of them: the show goes on. 'And how was it then?'

'It was . . .' This probably isn't the script Tom has

prepared. 'Well, it's been years since either of us . . .' He has to improvise. 'We had to work out how it all works, if you know what I mean, but then . . .'

Steven sets his smile, and plates on the table. 'What?'

'It's nice to fuck something that's meant to fit your cock.'

That gets Steven: the internalised homophobia of a lifetime in a sentence. With his back to Tom, he doesn't care if it's showing but keeps his voice even. 'You going to do it again?'

'Don't know, probably. Is that OK?' Tom sounds stunned to be let off so lightly.

Steven suctions the mask back on, turns to him. 'We'll have to have a threesome.'

Steven stalls at stage door, delaying the backdraft of emotion: through safety glass he can see her, smoking. All evening people have been weird with him. Like they know something they assume he doesn't. Like they're torn between feeling sorry for him and salivating over this new sensation. *A gay man and a lesbian! Imagine!* Steven is determined to get the joke on his own terms. Julie turns as he steps into the ring.

Phase one: disarmament. 'Great show!'

'Thank you.' She tightens her grip on the helmet in her hand, ready for battle.

'And great reviews!'

'Tom's just coming. I . . .'

'I'm not looking for him.' Phase two: seduction.

Julie hides her astonishment inside an exhalation, offers the packet to Steven.

'Why not?' He takes a cigarette. She leans in to light it; unnerved by his provocation, she succeeds on the second attempt. 'Thanks.'

'Hello!' Tom to the rescue, another helmet in hand.

'Hi!' Steven turns to face him, tries to keep down his inhalation.

'You're smoking?'

'Thought I'd try one.'

'You ready then?' Julie stubs her Marlboro in the gutter.

'Have fun!' Steven's hopes disappear around the corner with them. His fears remain with him. *Hell, why not?* He continues smoking, hears them laughing, then her motorbike speeding into the London hum. The nicotine, kicking in, craves alcohol for company. He can get at least two beers in before closing, if he hurries.

Steven has only once felt the urge to take advantage of his open-relationship, has never had the urge to take anyone back to his bedsit. But that night – *fuck it* – he needs a fuck and, in the morning, wakes sardined in his single bed with a gentleman whose name – Steven hopes – will pop into his pounding head soon. *What was he thinking?* Thinning hair, beard brushed with silver ... the resemblance stops there, doesn't go lower.

Some mornings later he's in bed again with the real thing, even initiates sex with him. His man. Except, really, he isn't. Steven can tell Tom's heart's not in it – even if his dick is – but is doing his best not to think about it, or who that dick has last been in, as he rodeos on top of Tom, his performance culminating in a cum shot that very nearly blinds the man.

Steven dismounts quickly, 'Sorry,' convulsing in that way he convulses when he's not sure whether to laugh or cry. Tom dries his eyes with the towel Steven hands him, doesn't dare open them. Steven takes this opportunity to pan his hands down Tom's toned body. Tom turns away from him, doesn't want to cum. And Steven knows then.

Blanketed in Tom's dressing gown, Steven's eyes start watering as the heat of his body raises the latent scent of the man-who-is-not-his-man to his nostrils one last time.

Tom emerges from the shower with towel about midriff, smells something different. 'When did you start smoking?'

'I thought you liked it.'

Tom ducks the bullet, it hits the Smeg. Steven fires another as Tom aims for the Gaggia.

'This isn't really working, is it?'

'No, I suppose it isn't.' Tom refills the coffee machine.

Knowing he won't witness it again, Steven finds the familiarity of this morning routine unbearable. 'I really love you.'

'You say that now.'

Now the gate is open, horse gone, Steven can't stop sobbing. 'Is this curtains then?'

'Let's leave it for a bit. See what happens.'

Blackness pours into Tom's cup. Steven will not be sugar on the side of it. 'No.' He stubs his cigarette. 'Let's not.'

The rest of the run is like a form of self-harm, seeing Tom shining in the curtain-lights every evening. But Steven refuses to hand his notice in, pull a sickie even: the theatre belongs to him as much as them. It's some consolation when the show doesn't extend, isn't the *something for everyone* as Dougie had planned; its last night tortoises around after an allotted three weeks and, somehow, they never meet face to face.

But now she's outside stage door again, as if taking a last

opportunity to taunt him. He hares straight past her, will not give her the satisfaction.

'I didn't ask him to leave you, Steven!'

He turns on hearing his name. 'You didn't have to.' She's given him a chance to deliver the line he's rehearsed so many times. 'I mean, why would he want my shit on his dick when he can have your vermillion lipstick?'

If she's shocked, she doesn't show it, takes a drag on her cigarette.

'All those men – they didn't matter one bit. But you . . . I couldn't compete.' Wrong equipment, but more than that. 'It's not just sex, it's . . .'

He's thrown off scent a moment, catching Tom watching from the safety of stage door. On seeing Steven seeing him, he disappears.

'A bit of fun.' Julie is crushing her butt under boot with unnecessary ferocity. 'Or it was meant to be.'

'Maybe for you. He's head over heels.' She looks at him like this is news. But it was obvious to everyone: Tom had got off on the transgression, then had fallen for the woman. Waters rising, Steven stakes his claim on a lost island. 'And he didn't leave me, I left him.'

Suddenly light snaps up on them. 'Everything OK?' Dougie is leaning from stage door, turning to Julie like Steven isn't there. 'Darling, we're just pouring the champagne.'

'Steven was just leaving.' Her fourth wall has been rebuilt in seconds.

Dougie holds the door to let her in. A slither of his former soft spot falls on Steven. 'Bye-bye, darling.' Then Dougie darkens the door firmly behind them.

When the thuggish thud of that final curtain stops

reverberating, Steven is swimming solo in the London hum. And as he heads out into it, his head music begins. *Here they come, the beautiful ones.* Bring them on. He hits Soho, beautiful as an open wound.

Soon there would be a new government. But now there would be a new Steven.

Nathan Evans is a writer, director and performer based in London. His poetry collection, *Threads*, was long-listed for the Polari First Book Prize, his second collection *CNUT* is published by Inkandescent. His stories have appeared in *Untitled: Voices*, *Queerlings* and the anthology *Mainstream*; his first collection will be published in 2022.

Gentrification – Cal Legorburu

It's after the roast and I'm straightening my back through the gloaming for home. 'Do you know this love's next sorrow?' mouths the darkness. Then silently, despite a Thamesian bone-chill tightening me, I am undone by the shame that I might not see everything as pregnable as you do. Tonight, we shot down sincerity and set upon its loose-limbed proclaimer, strewn up like the kids' piñata in a man's game. A boyfriend's tentative gesture of caring in an Instagram post, that bale of vulnerability smuggled in an eyeflash, yes, this saccharinity *must* be self-serving. For if not, we might endure towards his raw moment of feeling, away from its containment in derision and after swallowing the inhumanity we've been told we inhabit, tonight, all feeling was capitulation. But how long before this flat is an empty room of once-lovers, once-loved, we once knew? Who next, when we've festooned this crêpe paper beast to make his pleasure a penitence, and the party's become a dull edge? How the coke residue mottling his rainbow innards dampens our guises, wet with the effluent of engineered connection running off in toppled gin puddles: oily clouds over plastic empires; and whence the fairy lights lose their haste and the smoke rises, rises towards hell? I imagine you outside your hand-picked hive, surveying from its astroturfed piazza. And glimpsing back, my lips knowingly upturn to see your rings of smoky breath dance beyond the old wooden screen long after you leave, mouthing, 'I know, I know.'

———————————————

Cal Legorburu (he/them) is a British poet based between Dublin and London. His poetry has been published in *The King's Poet* and appraises the relationships between queer people, their literary genealogies and their experiences of urbanity. He is currently writing an MA thesis exploring chemsex in the neoliberal city.

The Split Woman – Marilyn Smith

I remember your dreams. A houseboat on the river. Nowhere too fancy, you said. Downstream at Laleham would be just fine. More affordable. Quirky even. There, moored beneath the lime trees and willows, we would have a little wiry terrier and a wooden terrace on which to read our books in deckchairs and sip red wine. As the sun dips to deepen the river to mottle green, you would bring out blankets to warm our legs and light candles at my feet. You showed me a picture once of a houseboat for sale online, and for a few moments I allowed myself to step into your wanderings. The best of both worlds, you said. We can jump on the tube at Hatton Cross to London anytime we like to catch a play or an exhibition. Then come home to our wooden house on the water to lie curled around each other, drifting into sleep as the moorhens and coots gurgle into the night. Be bloody cold in winter I'd said, and you'd given me that sad, knowing look.

Now I stroke your hair and I wonder if you know I'm here. Would you even know me? Three decades have passed since we split. No. *Split* is too incisive. Too clean. More like a slow, gradual splintering and painful wrench, leaving behind a jagged, angry wound in the shape of you. You are lying still, eyes shut. Soft breath barely sounding as I glance at the rise and fall of the white sheets across your chest. After all these years honey blonde still streaks across your pillow through the creeping grey. The nurse has stepped into the room to check on you. She is young and exudes a brusque busyness as she steps around the bed. I pull back my hand, a forgotten instinct from a long time ago. But what does the nurse care? Does she even see us? Two invisible old women. Two women who once ran laughing through the London rain, breathless and late as usual, just in time for curtain up. No time for pre-theatre cocktails. Fumbling and apologising past disturbed knees and tutting tongues to reach our discounted seats in the stalls. Our tilted faces lit by stage light; captivated by Carmen, or Don Quixote, or the sensual muscularity of the Tango dancers. Your furtive hand grasping mine under our coats as our pulses slow.

The nurse tells you she is going to bring up your pillow slightly to make you more comfortable. Do you hear her? Her voice is shrill in the emptiness of the room.

'There we are, my lovely. That's a bit better for you eh.'

An unmistakable Lancashire accent just like yours. I smile, remembering our old playful arguments about the warmth of Northerners versus the supposed froideur of the South. The nurse looks over in my direction before she checks the syringe driver. I stand and wander over to the window. Silver raindrops trickle down the glass as I look across the busy hospital car park to the sprawling retail park that lies beyond. On this wet April afternoon, grey figures with shopping trolleys rattle through the drizzle to and from a large supermarket.

I turn around as the nurse quietly leaves the room and I

come closer to you once again. Someone has positioned a hopeful bowl of fruit on top of the bedside cabinet, alongside a framed photograph of a cheerful white-haired woman kneeling beside a brown Labrador. Is this your wife, or a friend maybe? She looks kind. Perhaps it's her navy cardigan that drapes itself over the empty chair opposite, pulled up closely to your bed. I see she's been attentive in keeping your room neat and tidy. No evidence of the towering pile of books, or the scented candles and amulets that once adorned your bedside in Stanwell. Afternoons spent in your oversized bed, we barely heard the murmurings of the soul music, or the slow thrusts of the planes landing far beyond the perimeter road at Heathrow.

Something clatters from careless hands onto the floor just outside your room. A metallic clanging that reverberates through the hospital corridor amidst a flurry of muffled voices and stifled giggles. I look to your face as your eyelids twitch for the briefest of moments. You once said that *I* was careless. That I always broke everything; the delicate, purple champagne flute I placed too heavily into the sink, or the tasteless crystal vase your mother bought that I smashed while drunk, spilling red tulips and a little tide of water over the bedroom carpet. And then of course, there was your heart. I was careless as you said.

One summer's night on Old Compton Street, you clutched my hand boldly as I followed you through the afterwork drinkers spilling out of the pubs onto pavements. Wearing an open-necked black shirt and black jeans, strings of tiger's eye beads dangled from your neck. A clunky man's watch on your wrist. I sensed the Friday thrill on the evening air. It caught in the toss of your long hair and folded around your hips. The tall, tight T-shirted boys with their skinny jeans and long black eyelashes looked down at us over their cigarettes. Suited, leery straight men clutched pints and muttered lewd comments as we passed. I looked at the ground as my cheeks burned. You marched on, defiant. At fifty-three I guess you were done with the shame they inflicted. We kept on walking but I let go of your hand and slipped my arm through yours. That way we could pass for friends. It was safer, even in this neighbourhood. You stopped and turned to look at me. I didn't hold back; whined about how I struggled with it all. About my confusion. You and me? Well, maybe it was just a mid-life crisis, a phase I was going through.

'Maybe it's just love. Simply that,' you sighed.

'Look, let's go somewhere else. Where do you want to go?' I asked, hoping we could leave Soho and head to a quieter, less crowded place. Love wasn't that simple for me. I wasn't brave like you. That was my shame.

'I want to go home,' you answered and turned away.

On the tube you sat in silence, looking up at the adverts for car insurance and multi-vitamins. I watched your face next to mine, sinking in the dark reflection of the carriage window until you disappeared into the sky at Hounslow East. I guess I never did believe you. That one soul can split in two. And that when the inevitable heart-crushing separation occurs, it is as if two mirrors shatter into a million tiny shards. A lifetime spent running and chasing over the broken pieces, each one a stabbing, pointed reminder of all that is lost.

The afternoon is beginning to grow darker. Outside the hospital, the drizzle has turned to pelting rain. Your breathing is slower now. Heavier. A little louder. Notes of ginger and nutmeg float on the air. Is it my imaginings? No more the pall of sickness, but the scent of your favourite perfume. I remember how its spicy sweetness would remain in the softness of your dressing gown wrapped around my body, and linger in the hallway long after you'd left for work. I take your hand in mine. Don't care who sees. I've been waiting a while for you and it's time for us to go now. I know you're tired, the cold is beginning to creep through as the heat slips slowly from your fingers.

Shall we go to the river? We can take the yellow kayak from your shed. Dust off the cobwebs and grab the oars. I'll even pack a picnic for us. Halloumi wraps and green olives, and chilled Prosecco to drink from little plastic flutes. Let's lay the blanket on the river bank in the shadow of the syc-amore tree, and watch the mayflies dance. Lying on our backs we can gaze up at the sky and belly laugh, watching as the grey geese honk and bray through their noisy flight. Summer is returning as we glide our raft through the reed banks. Can you feel its warmth touching our soul? We find our balance, and slip once more into the gentle current. This time I'll take the oars, I know what to do now. We drift by the traveller children who stand waist deep, laugh-ing and splashing as they play. See the pink-shouldered lad ride his dappled pony into the water, holding the reins high as the children whoop and holler. We float by hazy water meadows and run our fingers through the ripples, stirring up the silty sand as the hermit crabs scurry for shelter. Can you see what is up ahead, my love? There, through the soft sunlight and willows the houseboats are waiting for us, holding the heat of the day within their wooden walls. I turn my face to you and we smile.

Marilyn Smith is from Liverpool, born into a family of natural storytellers. She now lives in Paris and enjoys writing short stories and flash fiction. Her work has appeared in Exeter Writers' Anthology, Radio Wey Magazine and Crew Radio's online blog. She has recently finished co-writing her first novel.

Man Dancing – Tony Peake

It was the morning of Alicia's party and because the sun had already cleared the roofs of the houses opposite, making his skylight sparkle, Fabian had little need of an alarm. But it soon began shrilling anyway. Next would come the phone, he suspected, since Alicia had called early on a number of occasions over the past few weeks to involve him in one party related decision or another. All unsuited, apparently, to being settled at a more convenient hour, later in the day. Or alone, for that matter.

Throwing back the covers, he swung his feet to the floor and rose to greet his reflection in the large, old-fashioned mirror that hung on the nearest wall. Happily, the sun chose this moment to disappear behind a cloud and he could see only a discreet approximation of his pyjamaed form as he stretched first one arm, then the other, above his head; bent backwards, sideways, forwards; extended a tentative leg; twirled an ankle; rotated his hips; blew himself a regretful kiss. If in your youth you've been limber – dazzlingly so – the sight of your morning self in middle age can be dispiriting. Indeed, Alicia had recently asked why he kept the mirror. She was aware, naturally, of its sentimental value, but was he really such a masochist?

What advice would she be wanting this morning, he wondered, as he headed for the kitchen area in the corner of the studio to brew himself some coffee. They'd dealt with the guest list, food, flowers, drink, lighting, music – pretty much everything, in fact, except what Alicia might wear.

Maddening Alicia! One of his oldest, dearest friends, and he owed her a great deal, but all the same – when it came to hogging the limelight, few could outstrip her. Or withstand the many other demands she liked to make. Expecting him, for instance, to not only advise about her party, but attend it too, despite his present aversion to socialising. And as for that bloody guest list! Wily old bitch.

On cue, the phone started its rendition of the music for Florimund's Act Three variation from *The Sleeping Beauty*, impelling Fabian towards the sofa, where he placed his mug of coffee within easy reach before making himself comfortable against the plushest of its cushions.

'Fabian *ici*,' he began. 'To whom do I have the pleasure?'

'Don't be coy,' responded Alicia. 'It doesn't suit.'

'You sound spry for someone approaching a milestone.'

There was a pause. Then, in steely tones: 'It's not a birthday party, dear. Not as such. As well you know. I've purposefully not mentioned advancing years to anyone and you're only in on the secret because . . .'

'We're so delightfully close?'

Another pause.

'I need your support,' she said eventually. 'Is all.'

'My support?'

'Yes, Fabian darling. Payback time.'

Later, once he'd showered and dressed, made the bed,

washed up his breakfast things and tidied away generally, he sat before the jigsaw puzzle he was currently working on and, as he slotted another piece into place, thought but yes, of course! *Payback time.* There was no doubting what he owed Alicia in return for her support of him. From ballet school onward, into his first job. Choice of further roles. Of companies. Even with Lawrence. There above all. How, towards the end, she'd proved indispensable.

He looked about the studio. At the sagging sofa; the bed that was far too big for only one person; the kitchen corner that couldn't possibly have accommodated more than one. And the mirror, of course, which reflected his loneliness back at him.

So maybe her wanting to involve him in the preparations for her party was simply another aspect of her continuing friendship? Maybe his attendance was required more for his own sake than for hers? Not because she wanted it, but because she thought he might. That barrage of old friends and colleagues, all inevitably asking: *How was he keeping? Why hadn't they seen him lately? He wasn't in hiding, was he?* With that look in their eyes as they remembered not to mention Lawrence. Maybe she thought he'd find this helpful?

The rest of the day had the feel of a first night. A slight tightness in the stomach. The ache of expectation. Too much watching of the clock. A restless siesta. Until, at seven sharp – she'd insisted he arrive early – he found himself on her threshold, ringing the bell.

The apparition who opened the front door did so with a slow pirouette that allowed him to take in and admire her chic dress (purple and black, Madam's preferred colours) from every angle.

'Well?' she asked with a teasing smile. 'Pass muster?'

'Her to a tee!' He smiled back. 'Where on earth did you find it?'

'Actually, she gave it to me. Not long before she died. But I'd never have worn it back then. Not my style. It needed time. Lots and lots . . .' Her smile became rueful. 'Of bloody time.'

Time which, he thought as he stepped into the hallway, has this evening turned a friend of many years into a version of the woman who'd given them their start in ballet and done most to shape their careers. Alicia did another twirl and it was Madam he saw before him, in her signature colours, tapping her foot to the music and waving a dramatic arm through the air as she demanded more of them.

Fluidity, mes enfants! Soften those shoulders! Yes, Lawrence, you too.

The expression on his face must have given him away, for Alicia grabbed his hand and said: 'Oh, Fabian! I know it's difficult. I know how it hurts. I was there, remember. But time, my love, time! Not always our friend, god knows, but it does march on and we have to keep step. Like in class. Under Madam. Missing a beat – not really an option, is it?'

Her words could not arrest the memories, however. Lawrence, lithe and suave at the barre, turning to appraise the new arrival as he walked in through the door. And in the rehearsal room mirror, a reflection of the hesitant new arrival in the ill-fitting sweater his mother had knitted for him and which Fabian still had somewhere, in the bottom of a drawer. Lawrence sitting across the table in the restaurant he'd taken Fabian to at the end of that first term; the sexiness of his fingers as they toyed with his glass.

The enticing green of Lawrence's eyes as he starts – oh, so slowly – to pull Fabian's sweater over his head. A junk shop through which they stumble, hand in hand and laughing, to discover a large, old-fashioned mirror against the far wall. Perfect, they decide, for the flat they're about to move into. Lawrence in the flat, lying sinuously on the bed and patting the sheet by his side. Then how tangled a sheet can become – and ultimately, how drenched with sweat. How stained by any number of bodily fluids, including shit. How happiness, warmth, care, understanding, love, security can be turned, like the twisted sheets, into a terrible travesty. Lawrence pirouetting from grace. Being dismantled bit by bit by a disease that knew no bounds until, in the end, nothing was left of him. Except some memories and a large, old-fashioned mirror.

'Courage, *mon enfant!*' Alicia was saying meanwhile. 'Think of me as Madam for the night. You're at the barre again. Well and truly in my sights. And my first require-ment? Some help in the kitchen. Those deft little fingers of yours have work to do.'

An hour or so later, as Alicia's rooms began filling with guests, Fabian stood with a replenished glass of wine by the kitchen counter, loath to move through into the eye of the party. More memories had been creeping up on him. Mainly of his boyhood self and the innocent hours he'd spent playing with his toy theatre, in which a collection of cardboard dancers had, at his prompting, seemed literally to fly through the air to the scratchy sound of Tchaikovsky on the portable gramophone player his parents had given him for his eleventh birthday. A cardboard *premier danseur noble,* a cardboard *prima ballerina* and a clutch of other, slightly less glamorous supporting figures, all of whom, in their adult, even more earth-bound incarnations, now lay in wait for him in the surrounding rooms.

How are you keeping? Haven't seen you lately. Been hiding?

Alicia came bustling by to demand that he help her carry through some canapés.

'You can't spend all evening in the kitchen!'

'I can't?'

'No, darling, you can't. Time to face the music.'

As he'd known would be the case, no sooner had he entered the living room than the questions started. Kindly, even warmly put, but always with that look in the eye as the questioner avoided any mention of Lawrence's death.

Except for Clive, their production manager during Fabian's last season, who said: 'Now listen! I've taken a villa on Mykonos for the summer. There'll be tons of room. And company, of course. Good company. Interested?' Which was about the closest anyone dared come.

He noticed a young man in the doorway, framed there as if in some advert for all that a person might ever crave. Youth, beauty, grace. You name it, the young man possessed it.

'Oh, my dear!' gasped Clive, eyes following the direction of Fabian's. 'Now *who* is that? I should come to Alicia's more often. We all should.'

Fabian couldn't help smiling at the way Clive had begun sucking in his stomach and was running a hopeful hand through what hair he had left.

'I'll have to ask her,' Clive went on. 'Here, let me take that. She's probably backstage somewhere.'

Relieving Fabian of the now empty plate of canapés, Clive vanished in the direction of the kitchen. Then a surprising thing happened. The young man was suddenly in front of Fabian, mere inches away, asking hesitantly: 'Excuse me. I don't mean to intrude. But it is Fabian, isn't it? Fabian Saunders?'

Cautiously, Fabian nodded.

'I thought it had to be. My name's Gary. Gary Todd. I'm a friend of Walter's and, through him, Alicia, of course. But then everyone knows Alicia. Alicia and her legendary parties. Though I've never seen you here before.' He blushed, thus heightening the effect of his astonishing beauty. 'I'm sorry. That sounded rude. I didn't mean . . .'

His discomfort was so touching, his beauty so searing, that although Fabian would ordinarily have ended the conversation there and then, instead he heard himself suggesting that they refill their glasses and find themselves a quiet corner in which to talk. Where, wine glasses charged, he began by asking Gary to tell him all about himself.

'Will you, please?'

'I'm not interesting.'

'Let me be the judge of that.'

So Gary told him, in stuttering detail, about being the only son of a policeman and a mother who tended to wrap her son in cotton wool. He spoke about his wretchedness at school, the awful bullying he'd experienced, his ultimate escape to London, the office job he'd found with Walter's dance company and how, as a result, he'd met Alicia when she'd come to talk to them all about her time as a ballerina.

He said: 'Do you mind if I tell you something?'

'What?'

The words came at increasing speed. Fabian, it transpired, had been something of a beacon to the boy. On his tenth birthday, Gary's mother had taken him to the ballet as his treat, where he'd seen Fabian dance Florimund. And in the course of this one performance, Gary had felt his budding sexuality crystallise. He'd always sensed his difference to the boys who teased and bullied him. Now he knew for sure. To experience Florimund as he had: this in itself told him everything he needed to know about himself.

At the same time, it had also given him a way of expressing what he felt. He could never have told his father outright. And by the same token, although he and his mother were close, he didn't dare confide in her either. She would only tell his father. So, what he'd done was profess a love of ballet. He and his mother had become major fans of Fabian. Seen him dance almost everything. Until, some years later, Gary had read an article in which Fabian had been interviewed at home about his life with Lawrence. Two dancers, living openly together. They'd been photographed standing, arms linked, before a large, old-fashioned mirror. And it was this image that had finally given Gary the courage to talk more fully to his mother about himself.

'And because it was you,' he said, 'her idol, it was actually fine. Not so easy with Dad, but again because of you, Mum really worked on him and, in the end, even he came round. Sort of. So you see: I owe you a great deal. And I wanted to thank you. I've been holding thumbs for ages that you'd be at one of Alicia's parties. And here you are at last! I hope you don't mind?'

'Mind?' said Fabian. 'Goodness!'

But here he was interrupted by Clive, who'd sidled up and was asking silkily: 'So are you going to introduce me to your cute new friend?'

After that, the conversation became desultory, others joined their group, the young man drifted away and when

Fabian eventually looked at his watch, he was surprised by the time.

'If you don't mind,' he whispered to Alicia, who was passing. 'I think I'm going to slip away.'

'Must you?'

'It's getting late.'

She laid a quick hand on his arm. 'Thank you,' she said. 'For your support.'

'The other way around, surely!'

Then Gary appeared at Fabian's side.

'Did I hear correctly? Are you leaving already? Can't I give you a lift?'

The question, slyly put, left no doubt in Fabian's mind that the offer might well involve more than just a lift. Considerably more. He glanced sharply at Alicia to see whether or not she'd noticed. Luckily, a peal of laughter on the other side of the room had distracted her. Someone else had clocked, though. The ever-watchful Clive, who said to Gary: 'You mean you have a car? What direction are you going in?'

'Actually,' said Fabian, looking directly into Gary's sky-blue eyes, 'on second thoughts, I think I ought to stay and help Alicia clear up.' He addressed Clive. 'And you're Hendon, right? Gary's quite the wrong direction. Aren't you, Gary?' Again he looked into those sky-blue eyes, seeing there a flicker both of understanding and thanks. Also regret? Or did he imagine that?

'It's been great meeting you,' he concluded, giving Gary a tight hug. The young man felt warm and supple in his arms. 'I won't forget this evening.'

'And there will be others,' said Alicia. 'More milestones along the way. If I have anything to do with it.'

The party didn't last much longer; but because Fabian had promised to help clear up, it was gone midnight by the time he ordered himself an Uber.

'You must wear that dress again,' he told Alicia as he left. 'It's most becoming.'

'She wasn't a total dragon, was she now?'

'We'd be nowhere without her. Absolutely nowhere.'

Then he was alone in the back of his Uber, being driven in silence through a silent suburbia. If he'd engaged in chat with the driver, he wouldn't have been able to continue savouring the evening. A beautiful young man stepping out of nowhere to offer himself. Who would have thought!

Back in the studio, the moonlight was flooding through the skylight in such a way as to make it appear that the figure reflected in the mirror, who then struck a pose, was that of a handsome young prince. Smiling, the figure struck another pose. And another. Seeming suddenly to fly free. Like that cardboard *premier danseur noble* from his youth. Airy and unconstrained, his whole future before him still.

Tony Peake grew up in South Africa, but lives in the UK, where he divides his time between London and north-east Essex. His books include the authorised biography of *Derek Jarman* and three novels, *North Facing* being the most recent. His short stories have been been widely anthologised. Further details: www.tonypeake.com

Fellatio, Regent's Park, 1989 – David Woodhead

I can't find the photo of us in our dungarees that day
in the zoo when we took acid in the reptile house
and you sucked off the guy who gave us dead mice
for the pythons that you flung at the

boy scouts who squealed in German or Italian
and we ran past lions and chimps and you tripped up
got up and spat in my face, you're a cunt, you said
but you loved me more than anyone else ever
    and we both

cried. The service will be on Zoom and it's
    donations in lieu
of flowers. Please write your memories or condolences
in the box below. I am sad because I'm not young and
I wish I'd made time for us, forgiven you, been kinder,

bold. I remember when we sat in the long grass,
looked out over London and everything was ours

David Woodhead PhD (he/him) is a gay man who writes poems and essays about queer subjectivities, recovery from addiction, and love. He is completing his memoir: *Writing Flowery for a Lad*. He is British European and lives in London and Scarborough, Yorkshire. @davestanpat

The Stages of Frostbite –
Margot Douaihy

Delirious, unleashed, snow pours through the seam of the storm-torn sky, white glued with mercury, crystal linen. Frost blinks its diamond eyes twice, three times, nine, like the glittering blue glass of a totalled car, the windshield shattered on impact. In the blizzard twilight, iridescent flame, neither day nor night, I think of your hand on mine, the outline of your body covering me completely, like the first snow of winter changing everything and nothing. Fox eye of quartz. Silver velvet. The skyline of New York stabbed the air like waveforms, frozen sound, thunder that never thaws. It sounded like this //>>///~~~.,^^^\~>(((((((^ Each snowflake the shape of an asterisk, the risk of *unsaid*. We knew it would shatter us, falling in love, we did it anyway. Left our husbands home, alone, said we were seeing a movie. Just two gals out on the town. *Sad movies make me cry*, the lady sings, *I don't know why*. Our affair, as invisible and dangerous as black ice on the sidewalk in front of the skyscraping hotel. *It's been so long* you said as you slid your fingers inside me. Did I mention how good it felt? Did I mention how, in high school, my friend Nina and I perched at the edge of the frozen lake and pressed our fingers to each other's necks (carotid arteries, I'd learn later), to see who'd pass out first. *It feels like dying*, Nina said brightly, her breath a frozen ghost bending backwards. *I don't want to die*, I said, *but being reborn would be all right*. I left earth for the length of a scream and woke up choking on blue light. *Sad movies*. I needed it then as I need it now – a woman's hand on my neck, traveling time, the tock goes tic. Frost bites when you're not careful. Our last night together, I was under-dressed as we walked to dinner. The moon, skull white, stubborn as a clock. A year later, your taste still laces my mouth – champagne, sweat, graphite. The storm hid behind metal, ready to pounce. *This movie with you*. In the gold haze of the hotel, heavy as the wedding ring I stowed at home, the leopard-mark dress slipped off my shoulder, you reached under me without warning. I wanted to push and push hard until the boat crashed iceberg cracked sea collapsed. *Make me cry*. What's it called? The storm women spark with our hands? A shared fever dream? Slow burn of frost biting. Lick of wind. Limn of need. The brain's striations cut fine as a record needle. *They remind me of you*. The song, the movie on repeat, changing every time it spins, and we're still there, two women burning, shivering like smoke in the cold white bed, both of us awake, unable to kill the show, neon glow. The untouchable moon, our secret carried across seasons.

*

get on top of me
we are both freezing to death
heat is our cure, curse

Margot Douaihy is a cross-genre queer writer based in Massachusetts, whose books include *Scranton Lace* and *Girls Like You* (Clemson University Press). Her work has been featured in *Colorado Review*, *The Florida Review*, *North American Review*, *Portland Review*, and elsewhere.

All Our Elastic Mistakes –
Laura Vincent

Meet me at the shipping container
Holding an orange
It tastes naked and cold
When you looked at me that day
I heard my own blood
Dress me in your clothes
We swap hats and ankle socks and ancestral curses
Trailing possessions across town
I learn to let go of ownership
I don't learn to assert myself
Why did you move to the suburbs
To eat someone else's noodles
It's so hard to be spontaneous
To get something going
You appear to me in dreams
Where you can't look at me
Under a sky the colour of milky tea
At midnight I searched in the whiplash wind
Your last message the torch

I crawled through the window
And slept in your bed
Only to find
I'm hopeless at geography
Do you think about the morning I woke to
    you cutting my hair
The mirror wouldn't meet my eyes
Ever since I've been sleeping longer and longer
Waiting for your scissors

Laura Vincent (Ngāti Māhanga) is a writer from rural Aotearoa. She has a fourteen-year-old food blog called hungryandfrozen.com, and her poetry and fiction has appeared in *Entropy*, *Peach Magazine*, *The Spinoff*, and the International Institute of Modern Letters journal *Turbine|Kapohau*.

Snowdrops in January –
Paul Whittering

It came to me in a flash of rare but fleeting self honesty –
the hopelessness of my love for Pete as I looked over at him
noodling away on his bass guitar, an Embassy red perched
delicately between his fulsome lips. Absorbed, beautiful,
radiant. His beauty all the more radiant for knowing not
of itself. Unrequited love is like a hunger that cannot be
sated. A delectable meal you can smell and taste yet never
eat. A meal you cannot consume. A love that cannot be
consummated.

The moment, a pristine, shimmering, lovelorn kind of
misery I can remember as if it were yesterday. Scarcely
admitted, this pain that had long formed a background to
my days now rose to a new intensity – like arthritic fingers
in January.

The likely date for the gig at The Riverside Inn Lechlade
was the 8th September 1988. Moz, one of our two singers,
ever the most organised in the band, has lovingly and pains-
takingly compiled a list of all our gigs from his diaries of
the time, including small annotations. No mean feat, as the

period stretches over four years and my band 'Shrink' played 238 gigs overall. As he says at the end of his email – 'Crikey, that took a while to type out!'

Setting up at the far end of the long bar of The Riverside Inn like a group of scaffolders assembling a stack, we were a hive of bloke-y activity – hauling the stuff out of the van, screwing mic stands to their bases, pulling the keyboards (I think I had three at this point) out of their artificial fur-lined flight cases which smelt strangely of vomit. The setting up of the drums, the amps, the lighting, the 'merch' table (we had mugs, badges, T-shirts and a 7 inch single), the placement of the PA cabs, the rolling out and gaffer taping of the multi-core that connected the sound desk to the audio cable junction box onstage.

It hit me like a truck – If I couldn't have Pete, I'm not sure I wanted to be alive. It's not that I wanted to die exactly, but more that the searing pain of this realisation was just too much to bear. It sounds so dramatic, but there you are. Because to be in love with someone you cannot have, who may or may not know how you feel, who may or may not share those feelings is one thing; but to have the burden of those feelings all on your own is quite another.

And then as I was screwing together the matching zigzag teeth of my keyboard stand, the intensity of the moment, the heaviness, the force, the bulk and heft of it started to move on – lugubriously, like a goods train passing through a station. My pain like a shipment of damp sweaty coal. But this stark unflinching acknowledgment had been an important message from the depths of me. What it said was that legitimate sexual desire and longing for someone, however distressing, difficult or inconvenient, cannot be ignored without destroying the person who desires and longs. And so perhaps this moment signalled the beginning of what was for me, to be a rather protracted and winding road towards my own sexual truth.

Being in a band, certainly in our case, is to spend large amounts of time just pissing about. I'm reminded of The Beatles on their American stadium tours in the old footage – jibing, joshing, riffing off one other like four parts of one indivisible whole – their own little Liverpudlian bubble which, amid the chaos of Beatle-mania surrounding them, appeared to form a type of protection. Being in a gang helps – it must have been a different story for the likes of Elvis, for Michael Jackson.

There are so many periods of down time to fill. The yawning chasm that separates the sound check from the start of the first set, waiting for the venue to close so you can get the gear out and load the van, getting to and from gigs. You piss about. Without it, the situation would be untenable. But, importantly, my true feelings could hide in plain sight under the cover of daftness. And pissing about with Pete – the wordplay, the accents, the buffoonery, was all in its way a kind of love making for me.

At home, as I write, the great puppeteer in the sky has contrived to put 'Rocket Man' over the airwaves, which comes dislocated and echoey from the builders' tinny radio in the next room where they work. Elton sings he's not the man they think he is at home; the song is about an astronaut, but could just as easily refer to a gay man trying to negotiate the perils of coming out. Hard enough now, but imagine that in the early seventies, and for such a prominent figure.

Around this time, we took possession of a very large and powerful 1970s PA system, which used to go wrong all the time, but luckily for us Phil the drummer was a dab hand with the soldering iron. The bass bins were each the size of a fat person's coffin. After this, came an A reg white, long-wheel-bass Ford Transit van and a new sound engineer in the form of 'Jeeves' (Phil Reeves) an engineering student (now a doctor) and friend of Pete's from Wootton Bassett.

One day on the street outside Moz's terraced house, I marvelled at Jeeves as workmanlike: he set about creating a partition and extra row of seating so that the entire band with kit could be conveyed all in one go – the van must have weighed a ton fully loaded with all of us inside. The narrow plywood bench seat remained, despite the addition of many cushions, unyielding and extremely uncomfortable. After a number of hours on the motorway, you would lose all sensation in your buttocks.

On journeys to gigs I developed a strategy to make sure I could sit next to Pete. Ideally in the front of the van. Feverish with anticipation, I was like a heroin addict before a fix – the strap of a tourniquet clenched between their teeth. The thing was, it all had to appear natural. As if I just happened to end up sitting next to him. So any sidling and manoeuvring, any last minute slipping into position, had to occur without jostle or elbows. In short, the process had to efface itself entirely lest I should be caught out and have my secret passion revealed.

On the rare times when this system didn't work, crestfallen, it would take me the remainder of the journey to get over it – on the inside I'd brood and seethe with jealousy towards my usurper, but outwardly did my best to cover that over – trying to join in with the banter, because in a band there is nowhere to hide.

You can be addicted to a person in quite the same way as

a substance. Mercifully, I gave hard drugs a swerve, but had I been exposed to them it may have been a different story. I have been, however, about as committed to booze, fags and shit chocolate as a person can be. What seems to marry them all is the lurch headlong towards the coveted thing – that formidable drive, the absence of any self control, of any choice, a sense of high alert and of danger that is as delicious as it is devastating. It is the allure of the forbidden fruit. Because these things have to be bad for you – to binge on kale or chia seeds makes no sense.

Pete to me was like heroin. The rush of pure elation as we set off to one gig or another with him at my side and the prospect of hours of close bodily contact, the crazed happiness that was perhaps more akin to delirium was something I have rarely felt before or since. Perhaps after all, it is the chemicals in the brain that get released upon contact with the thing, rather than the thing itself that we get addicted to.

It wasn't just a one-way street either. As young men of eighteen or nineteen we were like two lion cubs messing about amongst the pride, toying with each other, play fighting. Then, unlike with cubs perhaps (but who knows – are there gay lions?) things got sexy. It is curious how one tips into the other.

Ever fearful of rejection, of pushing things too far, of being noticed by the others, customarily I took my lead from Pete. I waited. Sooner or later if he was to my left on the passenger side, a wrist would dangle itself casually over my left shoulder – this delicious contact making something deep within me light up. And then ... and then ... his right leg would fold over my left one, now – the Blackpool Illuminations. Wow. Never would I risk such a bold move.

At this point I would have, probably we both would have had the most enormous erections.

Pete had a large penis of which he was quite fond, and used most tantalisingly to release it from its fly from time to time which he did once on one of these journeys. My word. There it was in all its veined, engorged glory. I had to get the van to stop, claiming rather glibly to need a pee and it was all I could do to contain the subsequent explosion by the side of the road.

And thus we'd cradle one another in this way – our bodies merging. Almost lovers. Not unlike Tantric sex perhaps, I would be, I think we both would've been, in a state of exquisite, sustained ecstasy until prising ourselves apart in a service station car park, when the spell would be broken as we all set forth in search of sweet tea and bacon sandwiches.

It isn't all peppermint breath and expensive cologne when you really, really fancy someone. It is also their filth, their body smells and secretions that get you going, and there was ample opportunity for that – personal hygiene being neither a priority nor something that could easily be maintained on the road for weeks sometimes at a time.

I shudder at the prospect of this revelation yet reveal it I must – we had a game. Guess the smell. Pete and I. It could be a scraping of skin cells from the crease of the nose held aloft on a fore finger, or behind the ear – both somewhat cheesy – or arse: pungent, musky, arsey. This game was played in the name of gross humour, but there was much more to it than that. I think for both of us, but probably I'll never know. Maybe I never should.

Sometimes we'd smell each other's breath, although this obviously wasn't part of the game. Oh, to smell his breath however metallic from cigarettes and lager. I'm blushing now a deep crimson – we used to smell each other's farts. How could a fart be sexy? Somehow Pete's were because I wanted him so badly. All that he was. I wanted to consume him and have him consume me and for us to disappear into that passion together forever. This was the dream, but it remained largely unexpressed, internal, and nibbled away at me from the inside like a necrotising pathogen.

Steering with the discomfort, I lay before you now a confession. It used to baffle me.

Sexual predilections are so confounding. Where do they come from? We all have them, and they I suspect are about as varied and strange as we are. Here it is – I like a bit of a belly on a man. Not perhaps the darkest of perversions, but a bit odd nonetheless. I've given up trying to figure out why. Perhaps it is as some like breasts. I'm not talking about a great shelf of blubber that hangs down to the knees (although doubtless there are those that like that too), but an incipient, pert belly, round and soft, that protrudes ever so slightly below the rib cage in a T-shirt.

The internet is many things both good and less good, but one thing I've learnt is that I am not alone in this, for both growers of bellies and those who admire them abound. A by-product of this discovery is that I feel less ashamed. And this is good, because so often shame is felt where it shouldn't be. Yes, you should feel shame if you kill someone, rob them, or hurt them with cruel words, but not perhaps if you have a simply less than standard sexual preference.

So Pete, as if he knew, maybe it was just the beer, grew a belly. We were packing up the van in the small hours after a gig at the Neptune theatre in Liverpool on the 13th July 1990 (thanks Moz), and that night would drive to Dover to catch a ferry to Ostend, before driving to Berlin and starting the first of three tours in the former East Germany.

This was the time of Jesus Jones, who I think had popularised the hoodie, and Pete was sporting a white one that hoisted up as he was lifting something into the van to reveal a perfect little belly. As time went on it grew a little more. He clearly liked his expanding waistline and with me watching would pull a certain expression, one of satisfaction as he rubbed it. That this ectomorph should grow a belly with which to taunt me – it is as if our old friend the great puppeteer had designed it this way. Perhaps for their own amusement.

What kept things going were those van journeys. The smell game. That belly. When, as was not infrequent, Pete held my gaze with those deep brown cow eyes for just a shade too long. The times he blew smoke in my face. The time, once, at The Old Fire Station Oxford before the gig he said under his breath as we passed between the van and venue 'I fancy you'. Bewildered, I think I said 'sorry'? And he said 'nothing'.

The time, alone, the pair of us in his parents' lounge (they must have been out) as we were getting ready for bed, suddenly coming across one another in our underwear – I can see us standing there for a moment, each drinking the other in – our beautiful young bodies bathed in soft lamplight. The time, possibly earlier the same evening on his parents' floral sofa when we watched *Invasion of the Body Snatchers* huddled together, conjoined in fear and excitement, all but embracing. And the time at The Spotted Cow Hotel in York when we shared a twin room, neither of us sleeping a wink, and how I felt him sitting up in bed looking at me, before in the gloom and through half-closed eyes actually seeing him do so.

Finally I came out. First to my sister over drinks at our local, who had been un-phased, which gave me some confidence. And then my mother, who'd overheard us talking at the kitchen table afterwards. Then the band. It was all fine. I'd told everyone in fact, bar Pete. It was clear at this point that we were going to go our separate ways – things had run their course. On the night of our final gig at the Park Hotel Swindon, after the soundcheck I asked Pete if he'd come for a quick drink – there was something I needed to talk to him about.

He took me on the back of his motorbike to The Rolleston, me encircling his leather-clad torso with my arms for one final embrace. Having bought us a pint, I spoke of my feelings for him. Haltingly, fearfully, ashamedly. He had looked shifty, uncomfortable and unmoored by my words because I wasn't joking. Our common currency was absent, and he was unaccustomed to this level of intensity, which evidently was too much. Because, and with irresistible shyness, Pete said how he was flattered, but that he wasn't gay.

In a parallel universe, maybe we kiss that time in his parents' lounge. Maybe more – devouring each other hungrily. Like feral animals. Like the tent scene in *Brokeback Mountain*. All the tumult of that withheld desire released. And one wonders how that outcome might have altered the course of our lives these past thirty years.

But in this one, the game was up. The extensive neural framework that had contained Pete in my mind – that galaxy of hope, desire and pain – was severed like a kind of psychic lobotomy in the aftermath. This was a kind of death, but also a sign of life returning – like snowdrops in January. As it turned out, the pain of keeping that hope alive, of clinging to the fantasy of having Pete fully was far greater than the losing of it.

Time heals. Freedom comes. New possibilities. Life to be lived. Love to be found. True love. Consummate love.

Pete found me on Facebook some years ago. In the then profile photo of me I'm standing under a waterfall in swimming shorts. 'I'd recognise that chest rug anywhere', he said. We exchanged a bit of chit chat, not a lot – he was never one to reveal much, which of course only added to the mystery way back when. I recited the first line of a Derek and Clive ditty we used to sing, 'as I was walking down the street one day . . .' and he replied with the next line 'I saw a house on fire'. This was unaccountably sad somehow. And in his last message he said: 'the Shrink days will always be the best'. For me, those few spare words betray a staggering depth of feeling.

As if on cue, Bonnie Tyler sings us out with 'Total Eclipse of the Heart'.

Paul Whittering began writing about his days in an early-nineties indie band during the first lockdown, after sustaining a knee injury from a misadventure with a unicycle. Paul lives at a partial building site in Peckham, south London which will soon, he hopes, become a beautiful flat. @WhitteringP

Melancholia – Tom Bland

sex isn't everything they say   others say sex is

a little death that erupts on a boat across a lake

i dream of being fucked on a floor that vibrates
         against rocks and exhaust pipes

*

everything queer is me   being queer makes me laugh
      i trip on a pill and feel love

*

remembering the break   my parents' divorce
i was too young to remember but my brother does
    the small details   i remember nothing

i sexualise my despair   i told this to a lover
he didn't understand   he recommended a therapist
in the middle of sex   i laughed

i broke his heart
            i never loved him

                    *

i trip on a pill and remember love but
            without a specific time or location
        but definitely a memory
the present never makes me cry

                        *

on youtube
                i tell everyone everything
            like anaïs nin   i admire her so much
                            i lie in bed
            she makes me feel desire is an eruption of soul
i
always believe in the soul   an autonomous creature
that either attacks or soothes

                        *

                        i used to fuck in public toilets
when i was young
sex was easy   emotion darting but never
                            staying

                    *

                i believe in god when it suits
love never suits   i only slept with men to begin with

mostly older ones

before my friend jumped on top

*

sometimes i wear a suit   the tie
            full of flowers   the flowers i am

> *my poetry teacher tells me to take out the flowers*
> *i want the flowers*
> *i want the clichés*
> *the whole of life is a cliché*
> *i feel it all the way through like blood*
> *on a drip*
> *into the sterile vein*

*

we had sex
against the tombstone we imagined
my life
your life
i can't tell them apart we are flowers

———————————————

Tom Bland's *The Death of the Clown* came out in 2018, and his new work, *Camp Fear*, a verse novel exploring sexuality, psychotherapy and gnosticism will be published in 2021. Both are with Bad Betty Press. He lives in East London.

How a Woman Howls –
Giulia Medaglini

The darkest hours of the night are earmarked, reserved for those too out of tune to mingle. The sleepless people riding the scent of solitude over virtual chats and repeatedly visited hyperlinks.

'What sound does a nosebleed make?'

I asked my music tutor once, to show her that some things she just didn't know. When she didn't reply I headbutted the piano's fallboard so hard a few drops of blood splattered her skirt. Outraged, she stomped her heels on my mother's Baluch rug and left the house trailing complaints behind her. A few weeks later, I heard she got married to her high school sweetheart.

*

The first half of my life I spent in a lukewarm prison of conforming womanhood. A part-time job to leave time for household chores, a decent flat where my in-laws had lived at some point but didn't deem good enough to age in, and a husband married on a whim – his or mine, I can't quite remember. I called him Yesterday because I never wanted to bring him into the present. Like something you try to forget but can't deny the influence of. He was the kind of man who would find gardening interesting only when the sun was out and the beer cold. No pretences, no pushing when I wasn't in the mood for sex, no remarks on my stern aversion to pregnancy either.

'Do you know how big a baby is?'

I said to him the only time he did bring up the topic a bit more insistently; index taut at a chopped watermelon resting in a cheap plastic bowl, soaking miserably in its drippings. Yesterday eyed the sliced fruit and winced on the sofa, bringing his attention back to the rugby match. He was an uncouth, albeit kind man, one of those who take the male duty of providing for their family as seriously as a full-time job. To know him was to know greasy burger joints and second-hand furniture shops. He had friends everywhere in the neighbourhood: the butcher, the clerk at our local mall, the mailman, the cleaning lady. Maybe that was the reason why I started to hate him – to dream of his beer-soaked intestines fraying under the pull of my fangs. Because of his people-pleasing demeanour and rough kindness, which clashed oh so loudly with my wilderness.

Winter was the worst season. My husband couldn't spend his days off in the garden and, as a result, meandered haphazardly around the house. To make things worse, at night he would wait until I was asleep and then cling to my back, breath damp-heavy in my nape. Every morning, as soon as I awoke and found him sprawled on my body, I would elbow him away and ignore the fleeting shadow of sadness palling his eyes. At some point in our married life, Yesterday must have figured out I didn't love him because he started going out with friends more and dozing off almost every night on the sofa. I, for my part, fell into this new routine rather happily; never once making an effort to save whatever was left of our facade of an average married couple.

'He's grown a belly, dear. Do you feed him healthy stuff? Thought you were vegan.'
    'Vegetarian, he likes his patties and fries.'

My mother-in-law was the epitome of treacle. If people could give you diabetes, my glycaemic index would have been doomed since the day I met her. Barely one metre and a half of hypocrisy, of the kind one could tolerate only for the sake of not ruining the Sunday lunch. I never blatantly hated her for her utter blindness to gender inequality or her attraction to luridly detailed gossip, nevertheless, her obses-sion for the wellbeing of her son gritted at my teeth like a nail on a chalkboard. She seemed under the impression that marrying Yesterday had somehow bestowed upon me the joy of caring for him like a mother, while the only thing it did was chop my paws.

'Still, dear, you shouldn't indulge him' she would repeat to me.

Funnily enough, the only time in my life that I did indulge my husband was when his mother died. The ceremony was sober and unexpectedly classy, bringing back memories of when my own mother had passed ten years before and of the dusty house she left me that no one knew the existence of. Maybe it was the resurfacing sting of guilt for the secret I was keeping from my husband, or maybe I felt sad for the passing of my mother-in-law, but when that night Yesterday crawled into the bed and latched at my breast with chapped lips, I let him. He cried the whole time he was inside me, thrusting a pathetic litany of *pleaseforgivemepleaseIloveyou* to which I didn't respond – not sure who he was talking to. The following day, I woke up and vomited in the sink. Yesterday helped me clean the mess and insisted on cooking some breakfast, all the while beaming with joy.

In retrospect, exploiting my husband's blind religiousness and general ignorance of basic biology wasn't the noblest of acts, but I was aching to be freed and at that point, an easy path was a temptation too great to resist. I knew a woman, down at the harbour market, who sold fake positive pregnancy tests for pranking families and friends and I slipped one in my bag of groceries that same day. My husband knew I never wanted to be a mother, and yet the idea that I would rather turn myself into an 'assassin' pulled strings I didn't know existed in him.

'I will get an abortion. Go find someone else to give you a family.'

Packing my things took less than an hour, as most of them were already lying in a suitcase under the bed – unconsciously waiting for the chance to leave. The last blow I threw at him on the doorstep was the push he needed to go feral. He kicked chairs and smashed potted plants, all accompanied by a pour of insults that felt like a refreshing shower. As if being displeased could give a retroactive justification to my lies and behaviour. Our neighbours peered from their doors at the commotion, but no one dared to step in. Fuelled by enthusiasm and relief, I hopped in a taxi and kept my eyes fixed on his figure shouting on the porch until Yesterday became no bigger than an eye floater. Then I laughed.

*

Quite a few things have stayed the same in my mother's house since I moved in. The Baluch rug with my tutor's heel still indented in the corner, my mother's wall-long bookcase of useless encyclopaedias, and my old computer. The OS is obsolete and the cooling vent buzzes like a dying wasp, but I can't bring myself to get rid of it. Each night – after coming back from work and gulping some overpriced Chinese food – I switch it on and dive back into my past. Into what I was before Yesterday.

The darkest hours of the night are earmarked, reserved for those people too out of tune to mingle. The ones like me, so happy in the web-woods that our usually unfitting nature melts around the edges of fandoms and forums. I grow mushrooms out of my spine to repress the wild me whimpering from my stomach; the desk chair a perfect soil to nurture the feeling that this is enough, this screen can suffice.

(Tomorrow_35) Do you ever wonder what's the sound of a bleeding nose?

I've never had a deterministic mindset; I'm pretty sure the miserable wed life I had was just the result of my craven choices, at the most, and not some fateful path laid in front of me when I was born. And yet the flashing question in the forum chat seems to possess the halo of more-than-coincidence around it, alluring and warm. I click on the username and start a private chat with the person I now feel so close to I barely contain the excitement.

(Shewolf) I asked my music tutor once, she didn't like it :)
(Tomorrow_35) I bet she didn't! Tell me more!

After I finish narrating my anecdote – every word so carefully selected as if I'm performing in front of a live audience – Tomorrow tells me her name and I squirm on the chair upon finding out that we live in the same city. We chat until the dead of night, until the mushrooms fall from my shoulders and all the things I thought I was interested in have become shapeless bags of bones compared to the thirst I have to know more of her. I go to sleep imagining the colour of her hair, the length of her fingers, the sounds she makes while cooking or showering and what God she prays to at night. I hope none.

My concentration at work is scraping the bottom, much to the dismay of my colleagues, who I suspect are one step away from filing a complaint letter to management. I push through emails and phone calls so quickly and unprofessionally that it feels like I'm trying to push time itself; to make it go faster to when we'll chat again. By now Mr Xiao and Mrs Wang, from the Chinese eatery, know me so well they have my food ready to pick up as soon as I step in – no matter if I get jammed in traffic and end up later than usual, they somehow know. Today is chow mein and dumplings day and Mrs Wang slides three fortune cookies down the bag for good measure, winking, almost motherly. I'm sure my mother would be pleased to know that I have someone happily feeding me. Never mind that I pay for my food and I'm probably the one who funded the new rice cooker.

When I finally get to my desk, Tomorrow is already online and patiently waiting for me to log in. The noodles disentangling under the steady crush of my teeth are a seam-less metaphor for our conversation – an escalator of words rolling on the screen, exposing ourselves bare to each other one inch at a time. I tell her of Yesterday with surgical minu-tiae, of all the years I've shredded into his casual misogyny, of the phantom baby I so resolutely murdered to free myself and of how he never once waited for me to sit down at the table before starting to eat. Tomorrow doesn't write much, doesn't take a stance and yet her replies have the sweet aftertaste of unconditional understanding. By the time I've caught her up on thirty-three years of life the dumplings' pastry is stuck to the box and I've lost my appetite. My fingers smell of old dust, skin's oils and faded plastic, and I lean on the chair to smell them, wondering if that's what a free woman smells like. Tomorrow would tell me if I asked her; just like she told me all the other secrets I dream of at night.

*

The darkest hours of the night are earmarked, and yet Tomorrow has shown me how to reclaim them for myself.

'Mr Xiao, I won't be having my usual on Sunday. I've got a date.'

The brown paper bag creaks joyfully under my fingers and

for a moment I forget to pay, but then Ms Wang glances at the husband flipping prawns on a grill and hands me a fortune cookie, and everything clicks back into place. *Today is the tomorrow we worried about yesterday,* it says.

When I later sit at my desk, a drop of blood slides quietly from my left nostril down to the upper lip.

Giulia Medaglini was born in Italy, now based in Scotland. Never fully belonging to one or the other, Giulia Medaglini is a bilingual writer who writes of queer themes and the overall struggle of not fitting in. Giulia has a degree in Biomechanics, but bones don't tell the stories she's interested in.

XXX – Libro Levi Bridgeman

When Mum dies, her face is as pale as a lemon. The back of her head is on the pillow. She dies slowly (Alzheimer's can be as incremental as rust forming on nails). Mum dies after thirteen days of no food or water. She dies in Room 20 of the Nursing Home, with her hoist and her wheelchair and her velvet armchair around her. She doesn't die easily – Mum was never easy after all. She dies with her breath breaking into a death rattle. She dies with her hair distended skywards like a white Demi-God.

When Mum dies, I am her only daughter.

1979

I'm wandering down the school corridor and I'm twelve. I'm wearing my uniform and I'm skinny and awkward-looking. I'm a bit chaotic. I don't have spots or tits or hips or periods yet. I'm not a fine example of femininity. But my best mate is. Melissa Evans is tiny and pretty with huge hazel eyes. And all the boys already fancy her. She's so alluring – she speaks with a gentle W for an R. She's like Pontypridd's

answer to Marilyn Monroe. And Melissa Evans never questions me looking raggedy and strange next to her. She just
thinks I'm cool. And she loves me. Melissa Evans holds my
hand as we walk down the corridor. And for her it's just
a hand-holding thing, but for me it's like a grenade going
off in my heart. And this femininity thing has never been
so marked as it is now. Before this age, age twelve, I could
be anything. It was allowed. I could climb trees and splash
in rivers and walk the dog in the woods for hours. No one
would question it. But now I'm twelve, I'm being told that
I need to be like Melissa Evans. Everything is colluding in
this – adverts, films, my family, Mum. I don't have a choice.
It's that or bust. And that's why I cling to Melissa's hand now,
because she doesn't tell me that. She tells me I'm OK. I'm
acceptable. I'm loved. That I don't need boys, or make-up, or
to speak with a W. She tells me that I can just be.

And as we turn the corridor, we face the blinding light that
is streaming in from the school's front door. And we start to
run now (even though we're not allowed to) Melissa Evans
and I start to bolt across the laminate floor. And our hearts
race and we laugh. But from this point, this laughing point,
everything gets much worse.

Because from this point, there is all this pressure.

And, at first, I try. I really do.

I buy dresses, I grow my hair, I wear heels, I put on lipstick,
I sleep with boys.

I try.

I really, really do.

1987

When I come out, I'm twenty. And I don't know any gay
people. Sinead O'Connor has just crashed onto the music

scene with her rage and her shaved head and her face as delicate as a deer. I'm listening to 'Troy' on my yellow Sony Walkman. And I don't know what to do. How to begin to be gay exactly. I flick through *City Limits* and head to the Lesbian and Gay section. My hands are shaking. I'm in Tufnell Park living with my brother. But he doesn't know yet. No one knows. I look at the gay list – the bars, the clubs, the groups, the meetings. My hands are shaking. I feel overwhelmed. I don't what to do – how to start – how does anyone start? Then I see an advert for volunteers at The London Lesbian and Gay Centre. And I reach for a pen and I circle the address in Farringdon.

Maybe I could wash dishes or hand out leaflets or work on the reception table. Maybe I could just blend in as a newbie gay.

Maybe I could be a credible baby dyke.

Maybe . . .

I'm really good at dating girls.

A week later, I end up stacking the chairs for the lesbian disco. I become really good at stacking chairs. Efficient. It gets a bit better. I buy all the right clothes. I wear Doctor Martins and 501s and bomber jackets. I cut my hair. I date girls.

But I still don't have a name for what I'm feeling. I don't have an idea what it might be called. The nearest things I hear are tomboy, androgynous, hermaphrodite.

I don't have the language. I don't feel female, but I don't feel male either. I'm kind of in between. But I carry on with the charade because it's easier. We're told this. It's easier to just continue.

girl / boy / woman / man: the constructs of gender.

It's pretty comprehensive.

2019

I'm standing in my bedroom alone. It's December. Mum died six months ago and Dad died five years ago. And I don't have any family. And up until this point it hasn't really hit me.

I'm an orphan.

I have eleven copies of this deed poll form in my hand but I don't need them all. Eleven is excessive but that's how many I have. In the envelope, they've given me the list of people who need to be sent the form.

The form has to go to my: bank, passport office, DVLA, doctor, dentist, tax office, place of employment.

It's the strangest feeling. It's liberating but unknown. It's such an elemental thing. A name. A pronoun. I don't know how I feel when this deed poll form goes into the world because it means people will be referring to me in a different way. I will be different. I will be a phantom or a spectre. A ghost even to myself.

It'll be easy for new people to see me in this way.

But what about the pre-existing people, what will they see?

I ask my friend and he says, 'Choose a name that is magical and mighty.'

And suddenly it's all making so much sense.

Time – past, present, future.

There's a coalescence of sound and fury and light.

I've tried so many different name versions. Made so many lists. I didn't know which iteration to choose. But now I feel that I've found it.

When at last I do choose one, I start updating my social media, I go on Facebook. It goes into some kind of meltdown. I get over 250 loves for my new name. People are very enthusiastic. And I feel a little bit scared and a little bit sick.

It's 1979 and I'm running down the school corridor. It's 1987 and I'm flicking through *City Limits*.
It's 2019 and I'm holding my name-changing deed poll and Mum is dead and I'm crying without the capacity to stop. But I say it out loud for the first time. Then I send it to myself in a text.
Hello,
My name is Libro Levi.
And I am Non-Binary.
Xxx

Libro Levi Bridgeman is a European writer based in London and has written for the theatre and BBC Radio 4. They have a PhD from UEA in Creative Writing where they were awarded the HSC Scholarship. Published short stories include: Gregory (*Brand Magazine*) and Letter To My Future Lover (*F, M and Other*, Knight Errant Press).

Libro Levi co-runs Hotpencil Press with Serge Nicholson. Publications include: *There Is No Word For It* (2011), *The Butch Monologues* (2017), and *Letter To My Little Queer Self* (2021).

Libro Levi is currently working on a novel. They teach Creative Writing in Guildhall Drama School and Imperial College and have taught in five UK prisons.